CAROLINE
and the Seven Little Words

CAROLINE
and the
Seven Little Words

by MIRIAM E. MASON
Illustrated by Paul Frame

THE MACMILLAN COMPANY, NEW YORK
COLLIER-MACMILLAN LIMITED, LONDON

jM 386 cat

LOVINGLY DEDICATED
TO ALL OF
CAROLINE'S FRIENDS
EVERYWHERE!

Also by Miriam E. Mason

The Baby Jesus
Becky and Her Brave Cat, Bluegrass
Benjamin Lucky
Caroline and Her Kettle Named Maud
Freddy
Hoppity
Katie Kittenheart
Little Jonathan
The Major and His Camels
Matilda and Her Family
The Middle Sister
Miney and the Blessing
A Pony Called Lightning
A Small Farm for Andy
The Sugarbush Family
Timothy Has Ideas

Contents

"I AM GOING TO BE A DOCTOR"

1. Caroline speaks up

As SHE walked over the long road to school that morning Caroline Gray made up her mind about something.

"This morning I am going to speak up," she promised herself. "I am going to tell. I have a right to tell, even if I am a girl!"

She looked at her five young uncles striding along ahead of her through the woods. They had already spoken up. They had told what they expected to do when they were men.

Mr. Nicholson, the new teacher at Pigeon Roost School, had called on four of the boys so far and listened while they told about their goals in life. He had nodded his head and encouraged each boy.

Caroline had a goal in life, too. She knew what she wanted to be when she was a woman. Though she was not quite eleven yet, she knew exactly what she intended to do when she was grown up.

But Mr. Nicholson never called on Caroline to ask about her goal in life. Never once did he say:

"And what do you intend to do when you grow up, Caroline? What is your goal in life?"

"This morning I am going to hold my hand up high," Caroline promised. "I am going to hold it up high until Mr. Nicholson lets me speak."

Caroline and her family had been pioneers in Michigan for almost three years.

Back in New York State the Grays had lived in a small town called Gray's Crossing. Caroline's father was part of a rather unusual family. There were eighteen boys in the family so Caroline had seventeen uncles.

Caroline's father was one of the older boys and he had many little brothers. So Caroline had several very young uncles; some no older than she was and some even younger.

When Caroline's father decided to leave New

York and come to Michigan as a pioneer he brought along five of his younger brothers.

"A new land like Michigan needs lots of boys," Mr. Gray had said. "And you boys in Gray's Crossing need more room."

Caroline looked at her five uncles leading the way along the woods road.

"A girl with five uncles has plenty of protection on the way to school," she thought. "Though I sometimes wish they did not walk so far ahead of me and act so bossy!"

Steven was seventeen and he was really a young man, taller than Mr. Nicholson, the schoolteacher. John was fourteen. Henry was twelve. Robert was ten and David was only eight. But even the youngest uncles acted big and bossy around Caroline.

They never allowed her to forget that she was a girl and they were the men of the family.

"A nice dog would be company for me and would walk along behind me," she said to herself, walking along behind the boys.

Just then Uncle Robert cried "Ouch!" He put his hand over a torn place in his shirt. "Drat you, anyway, you yellow-bellied sapsucker!"

A big hornet, bad tempered and half drunk from the juice of the wild grape cluster where he had been perched, had stung Uncle Robert. If Uncle Robert had not been walking backward trying to imitate a prancing horse he would not have bumped into the grapevine and disturbed the hornet.

The sting of a hornet is extremely painful so none of the others scolded Robert for his loud roaring. Uncle Steven thumped the hornet off into space and remarked that a big red welt was coming on Robert's shoulder.

This was no news to Robert, who was now prancing up and down with pain while tears ran down his cheeks. To keep from crying like a girl, Uncle Robert was shouting all the violent words he knew, and he knew several.

The other boys just looked at him in a rather helpless way. Uncle Henry almost choked on the apple he was eating and then roared at Caroline, "Well, why don't you do something?"

"Just hold your horses," Caroline answered. "Hold your horses and get a handful of mud. Robert, stop jumping and swearing. John, hold his shirt away from the sting. Steven, look out for other hornets! David, get out of my way!"

Her uncles obeyed meekly, for Caroline could be bossy when she needed to be. She looked at the big red welt and saw the hornet sting sticking up in the middle of it. Her small, slim hands were just right for the job.

She caught the tiny sting between her finger and thumbnail and pulled it out. Then she covered the big red swelling with cold black mud which Uncle Henry brought from a nearby puddle.

"It feels better already," said Robert, ready to prance again.

"I'm not finished. Stand still!" ordered Caroline.

She took from under her collar the threaded needle which she always kept there. She pulled the torn edges of the shirt together and sewed them.

The big lump of mud on his shoulder gave Robert a funny shape, especially when he held his hand over it as Caroline had commanded him to do. When the mud dried it would make a good plaster.

Soon Caroline and her uncles were in their places in the schoolroom. Mr. Nicholson rang a bell and shouted, "Books! To your books!"

He was young, not much older than Uncle Steven, and he was small and thin. His clothes were rather ragged.

But he had a loud voice and a stern manner and when he looked at his scholars and spoke to them they were very respectful.

This morning he stood in the front of the room looking out over the pupils. His arms were folded across his chest and his greenish-brownish eyes were very watchful.

Silence settled down over the room. Josiebell Jones and the other big girls stopped their giggling. Not a boy in the room whistled or dared put a grasshopper in a girl's hair.

Caroline could feel her heart beating very hard. She wondered if the others in the schoolroom could hear it. But nobody looked at her. Everybody was looking at Mr. Nicholson.

When the room was so quiet that you could hear the wood mice running and playing in the log walls, Mr. Nicholson spoke. His voice was not like the rest of him. His voice was big and loud and as deep as a bullfrog's.

"Now we will continue to discuss our goals in life," said Mr. Nicholson. "Who wishes to speak?"

A few boys who had not yet told their goals held up their hands. Instantly Caroline held up her hand. Not another girl in the room did so.

Mr. Nicholson overlooked Caroline's hand though it was high in the air. Instead, he called on Uncle David, who did not even have his hand up because he was a rather shy boy.

Caroline kept her hand up all the time David was telling how he intended to be a rich merchant when he grew up. Once he got started he talked quite awhile, telling of all the different kinds of candy and toys he would have in his store.

Mr. Nicholson finally said that would be enough for this time and he was sure that many people would enjoy a candy and toy store. He still did not call on Caroline, whose arm was getting a little tired. He called instead on a very talkative boy who had been waving his hand and snapping his fingers.

Everybody listened for a few minutes while the boy told how he meant to be a famous poet when he grew up and recited some of the poetry he had written.

Caroline's arm was so tired by this time that it was beginning to droop like a cornstalk in the wind. Her five uncles frowned at her. Uncle Steven made signs she should put her hand down. Uncle Henry made signs she should keep her mouth shut. Uncle

Robert leaned forward to give her a little poke and the mud on his shoulder slipped off and down his side, tickling him so he could only giggle, causing the teacher to look at him sternly.

Caroline paid no attention to her uncles. She kept her eyes on Mr. Nicholson's face.

When Caroline made a promise she kept that promise even if it was only to herself. And she had promised herself this morning that she was going to speak up and tell her goal in life.

At last Mr. Nicholson spoke to her.

"Did you want something, Caroline?" he asked. "Were you wanting to be excused or get a drink of water?"

"I am wanting to tell my goal in life, if you please," answered Caroline politely but firmly.

"You may tell," said the teacher kindly. "Though of course we already know that your goal in life is to be a fine cook and housekeeper and a good wife and mother."

At the thought of Caroline being a wife and mother several of the boys in the room burst into loud laughter. Mr. Nicholson looked at them and they became silent and respectful.

[9]

"Being a good wife and mother is not my goal," said Caroline. "I would like to tell my real goal."

"Very well, we will listen," sighed Mr. Nicholson.

So at last Caroline spoke the words which she had promised herself to speak. She spoke them in a loud clear voice which trembled a little because she was so excited.

"I am going to be a doctor," said Caroline.

All the other pupils turned and looked at her in amazement, so she felt she had to keep on talking.

"I am going to be a real doctor with a bag full of medicine," she insisted. "I intend to have an office in Pigeon Roost Village and to visit the sick on a fiery red colt followed by a faithful watchdog."

There now. She had spoken. Caroline folded her hands in front of her and sat up very straight. She had said what she had promised to say.

Some of the boys began to laugh and then the girls joined in and soon all the pupils were laughing like mad except Caroline's uncles, who looked terribly ashamed.

On the way home the boys scolded her, because they were embarrassed.

"Why must you be so different from other girls?"

complained Uncle Robert. Uncle Henry said bitterly, "It is a wonder to me you did not want to be a preacher like Brother Carpenter and ride through the woods preaching sermons! Why don't you be a preacher?"

"Because I prefer to be a doctor like Grandfather Howard," answered Caroline calmly. Grandfather Howard was her mother's father, who lived back in New York State and was a very fine doctor.

"It is still a crazy idea," insisted Uncle Henry, gnawing on a leftover rabbit leg from his lunch pail. "Who ever heard of a girl doctor, especially in Pigeon County? What if you had to ride through the woods at night? What if you had to cross the river to pull somebody's tooth?"

"What if you had to cut off somebody's leg?" growled Uncle David. "Doctors often have to cut off people's legs."

"Caroline cannot even cut off a chicken's head," laughed Uncle Robert. "Not even when the preacher is coming for dinner and she knows how the preacher loves chicken and dumplings!"

Uncle Steven spoke up for Caroline.

"You are not such a famous wolf killer yourself,"

he said to his young brother. "And who can make a better dumpling than Caroline after the chicken is killed? And also, who took care of your hornet sting?"

Caroline looked at him gratefully. Sometimes she felt that Steven was her favorite among the uncles.

"I am glad you like my chicken dumplings," she said. "And you helped with the hornet, too. It was you who thumped him off with your bare fingers. And when I do grow up and become a doctor with a medicine bag and a fiery horse and a fierce dog following behind, you may be sure you can count on me if you are sick or shot with a gun."

She would have gone on talking but Steven smiled and patted her shoulder and reminded her that the Bible said women should keep silent when men were present.

"Of course you have already broken the rule, but everybody makes some mistakes," he said kindly. He then preached her a short sermon about how women should behave, especially women not quite eleven.

Caroline listened politely, for she knew that Steven liked to make speeches. As soon as he had fin-

ished his sermon, she offered to race with the boys
to the old hemlock tree away up the road.

She was very swift-footed and was soon ahead of
the boys. No doubt she would have won the race,
but just as she was ready to touch the old tree and
cry "Home Free!" she saw an enormous black snake
stretched across the road which scared her so she
turned and ran the other way.

"You see?" said Uncle Robert. "Just suppose you

had been a doctor and somebody was dying and a snake got in your way?"

"What if it had been a rattlesnake or a copperhead?" added Uncle Henry. "Then *you* might have been the dead one."

Uncle David quickly made up a rhyme:

"Dr. Gray, run away,
   Because a snake is in your way!"

"Enough is enough," said Uncle Steven sternly. "Any one of you who mentions this at home this evening will get a thrashing from me. Caroline has been punished enough for her foolish words."

"Foolish words they may be," thought Caroline to herself, "but I still intend to be a doctor when I am a woman!"

But now more pleasant thoughts came riding along on the evening breeze. A smell of freshly baked bread and good fried meat drifted through the air. A few steps more would bring Caroline and her uncles in view of the fine homestead in the big clearing.

Soon they would all be sitting around the supper table eating delicious hot bread with butter and apple butter. They would be munching brown crisp spareribs and the mealy white potatoes which grew so well in the Michigan soil.

"And I *think* I smell a cranberry pie!" Caroline said, sniffing. "A cranberry pie made with maple sugar!"

She was so glad her mother was the best cook in Pigeon County.

2. Brother Carpenter's sheep

"THERE's company," called Uncle Henry, who was still in the lead. Then he added in a joyful tone:

"Brother Carpenter's here!"

The Grays were always delighted when Brother Carpenter stopped to visit them and so were most of the other families in Pigeon County. He was a young man whom everybody liked to have around. Not only could he preach very good sermons and read from the Bible in a beautiful voice, but he could sing so loud that he could be heard from a long distance.

Nor was that all he could do. He could make very good johnny cake and excellent soup. He knew what to do for the sick, and when he visited homes where the mothers were sick he would set to work and clean up the house and wash the clothes as well as a woman.

Besides he knew many jokes and stories and games.

"Oh, I do hope Brother Carpenter can stay with us for days and days!" cried Caroline. All her uncles agreed with her, but it was not a very strong hope. Brother Carpenter was so busy he never had time to visit anybody for long at a time.

"I must be looking after my sheep," he always said. By sheep he meant all the people in and around Pigeon County.

In a minute Caroline and her uncles saw that Brother Carpenter was not the only company.

Down by the barn, not far from Brother Carpenter's prancing black horse, were a pair of thin, tired, shaggy oxen. They were still fastened to a battered old wagon.

In the front yard a sad-looking man was walking around with Caroline's father and Brother Carpenter. Two wild and dirty boys about the ages of Uncle Henry and Uncle David were tagging behind them.

Brother Carpenter came out to meet the home-comers, leading a boy by each hand.

"These are the Walker boys," said Brother Carpenter with his big, cheerful smile. "Their names are Lewis and Horace and their home is down by the marsh."

"Not any more it ain't," grumbled Lewis. "We're on our way back to Ohio."

As if he had not heard Lewis, Brother Carpenter went on talking.

"Their mother and sisters are in the house; two fine girls named Dorcas and Lydia."

"The twins are in the house too; they're sick in bed with the shivers and shakes," muttered Horace. He added gloomily, "We've all had the shivers and shakes and toothache and the itch besides!"

"Caroline here will be a great help," promised Brother Carpenter. "She has a way with the sick!"

"It'll be fun to have some girls for company," said Caroline happily and hoped that the girls did not look like their brothers.

But she was disappointed when she went into the house and saw Mrs. Walker and her daughters, Lydia and Dorcas. If anything they looked more gloomy and dirty and ragtag than their brothers. They did not smile back when Caroline smiled at them.

"We hate Michigan," said Lydia. "We're going back to Ohio."

"Michigan is nothing but a great big woods full of snakes and spooks and wolves and wildcats and horse thieves," added Dorcas.

Caroline's cheeks turned pink and she thought that this was not a very polite way to talk, but she managed to hold her peace and ask about the twins. Maybe *they* would be more friendly.

"The poor little things are in bed," said Caroline's mother, bustling cheerfully about with her supper-getting. "They are too miserable to travel any farther. Something to eat and a good night's rest will do wonders for them, however."

She dipped up a bowl of soup and handed it to her daughter. "Feed the little ones, Caroline," she said. "Be careful not to spill the hot soup on them."

And she gave brisk orders to the boys.

"Bring the bread and pies from the outdoor oven, Henry. Robert, go to the springhouse and get a crock of morning's milk. David, fill this bowl with some of the new cider apple butter from the store-house."

"Women's work," whispered David, glaring at the woman company sitting there and doing nothing to help.

"The twins are named Rosie and Roger," Mrs. Walker informed Caroline. "They're real mean kids on account of living in such a desolate land as Michigan."

3. Wildcats in the bedroom

CAROLINE took the bowl of soup and went into the bedroom. She had fed many a hungry orphaned animal, even a baby wildcat whose mother had been killed. She had even saved the life of Brother Carpenter's pet lamb when it was a starving orphan.

Brother Carpenter had praised her and said that she had a great skill with sick and frightened young creatures. It was his praise which had really given her the idea of being a doctor when she grew up.

But the two small children who looked up at her from Mrs. Gray's bed were wilder than wildcats and fiercer than red-tailed hawks.

"Go away!" screamed one, and the other howled, "Get out!"

Their faces were very red. Caroline could tell they had fever and were maybe out of their minds.

"I have good, good soup for you," she said in her kindest voice. "It will make you feel better."

Holding the bowl of soup in one hand, she put her other hand gently on Rosie's forehead to stroke it.

"There, now!" she said, trying to sound comforting and kind, as a good doctor should.

Rosie grabbed Caroline's hand in her rough little paws and bit her fingers as hard as she could.

"Ouch!" cried Caroline, pulling her hand away. She forgot the soup in her other hand and it fell on the bed. The twins howled like wolverenes as the hot soup soaked through the blanket onto their legs.

"At least I saved my fingers," thought Caroline, tears of pain coming to her eyes. She reached over to pick up the upside-down soup bowl from the bed and her long black hair tickled Roger's nose.

Instantly he grabbed it in both hands and yanked as hard as he could, still bawling at the top of his voice.

Caroline slapped his hands sharply and got her

hair loose from his hands. For a child so sick, he seemed very strong.

Both twins began to kick along with their screaming. Rosie threw the bowl at Caroline and Roger grabbed the spoon and threatened her with it.

"You leave us alone!" they screeched. Caroline now added her own sobs to the screaming. The noise brought Mrs. Gray, Mrs. Walker, and the girls in.

"I was only trying to help them," wailed Caroline. "But they don't *want* to be helped!"

"They're real mean kids," said Mrs. Walker.

"That's because they've been scared to death all their lives."

She went over and gave a sharp slap to each of the small children. "You kids be thankful and shut up!" she ordered them.

The twins' screeching changed into a small, sad whining.

"She hit me!" sobbed Rosie, pointing to Caroline. Roger added, "She poured hot water all over me!"

"I did no such things!" Caroline defended herself. "I was trying to help you but I'd rather take care of a wolverene!"

Dorcas and Lydia looked at Caroline with unfriendly faces, and Dorcas muttered something about "picking on somebody your own size to fight with."

Caroline shook her fist at the growling girls.

"Take care of your own mean little sister and brother," she cried. Her fingers still ached and she saw several of her black hairs in Roger's hand. "They don't even act like *children!*"

"I'm hungry," whined Rosie, and Roger whined, "I'm hungry too and I hurt."

"It's their own fault," declared Caroline. "And I'm hungry, too, and I'm going to eat my supper. You can stay here and yell!"

"Caroline!" reproved her mother in a gentle, but firm tone. "That is no way to talk to a sick child!"

By this time Uncle David, who liked excitement, had come in.

"Now you see!" he whispered to Caroline. "I told you. First it was a snake you ran from. Now it's two little sick kids in bed."

"All of you come out now and let the children rest," commanded Mrs. Gray. "It's time to eat."

She looked closely at David, who had just made up another rhyme. He was whispering:

"Oh, Dr. Gray, do not stay,
   Save your life and run away!"

Caroline spoke up.

"Somebody should look after the twins and wash the soup off them," she said. "I will do that. I am *not* afraid of them."

Her mother gave her a smile which made Caroline feel good all over.

"David will be glad to help you," said Mrs. Gray. "David always likes to be helpful. He will help wash and feed the twins."

David looked so gloomy that Caroline could not keep from laughing a little. She decided she could make up a little poem, too.

"David, David, please come quick,
These little lambs are awful sick!"

"The twins are in good hands," said Mrs. Gray cheerfully, as she led her company out of the bedroom. She dipped some warm water from the big iron kettle and gave it to David, who had followed.

"Be very careful not to spill the water," she said. "Remember, it all has to be carried from the spring."

David came in holding the bowl of warm water carefully.

"Yellow-bellied sapsuckers!" he muttered. "Hog-nosed rattlesnakes! Dirt-colored tiger beetles!"

"You really know lots about nature!" said Caroline as she washed the hot faces of the twins and their grimy hands.

This time the twins did not bite or pull hair or scream. Maybe they were afraid of their mother or maybe they just liked the feeling of being clean and cool.

When the washing was over, David offered to bring in some milk and help feed the children. He held up each child's head while Caroline spooned the cool sweet milk into their mouths.

"Soon you will feel better," she promised. "Cold milk is good for little kittens, little dogs, little lambs, little wildcats, little pigs, and little children!"

"Already they're asleep," said David proudly.

4. A most unlucky family

THAT evening Caroline and her uncles learned a little more about their visitors. Brother Carpenter told them as he helped Caroline and the boys with the evening chores.

They were a very unlucky family. They had spent years traveling around in search of a good home where they could settle down and be happy like other people.

"But every place they go they have bad luck," said Brother Carpenter, loading his arms with wood for the kitchen fire. "If they travel by boat a storm comes up. Burglars stole from them in the city. Sile

Doty, the horse thief, robbed them of their fine horses. And when they finally came to Michigan the only place they could find to live was that homestead away back in the marshes where *nobody* has ever stayed."

"Things were not easy for us when my brother came from New York a few years ago," said Uncle Steven sternly. "Pioneers expect to have hard times. My brother warned us of that before he brought us out here."

"Some people can stand hard times better than other people," said the preacher kindly. "It is our duty to help those who need help. Your brother has a fine homestead on good land. Your mother, Caroline, has the finest kitchen in Pigeon County and lots of good food to cook in it."

But the Walkers' homestead back in the marshes had been a miserable place where nobody stayed long.

There was no kitchen to speak of and rats ran wild in the house, stealing what poor food the Walkers had and biting the children's toes at night. It was really no wonder that the Walkers had made up their minds to leave.

Brother Carpenter did not want the Walkers to leave Pigeon County. That was why he had brought them for a visit with the Grays.

"When they see how well you are doing, perhaps they will be persuaded to return to their homestead, try a little harder, and grow into fine Michigan pioneers," said the young preacher, leading the way into the house with his great armload of wood.

In the cozy big kitchen Mrs. Gray was scouring the supper kettles while Mrs. Walker sat in front of the fire and told about her backaches and other pains.

Out behind the house Mr. Gray was digging a deep hole in the ground where he would bury the apples and potatoes for winter. Mr. Walker was sitting on a tree stump telling about his adventures with the famous robber Sile Doty.

Lewis and Horace, Dorcas and Lydia were quarreling about something that did not really matter to anybody but caused a good deal of noise.

"You can see the children need schooling," said Brother Carpenter. "Perhaps you can take them to school with you next week. They might turn out to be fine scholars."

Caroline looked at the Walker children. She did not feel so hopeful about them as Brother Carpenter seemed to feel.

But Brother Carpenter was a very hopeful man. Where many people would have given up, he kept on trying, whether it was trying to get people interested in school or trying to find somebody's lost cow. In fact, the word "try" was one of Brother Carpenter's favorite words.

"Will you listen while I say the multiplication tables?" Caroline asked the young preacher when the evening chores were done. "It is the tables of seven, and they are very hard for me."

Brother Carpenter agreed cheerfully. They walked out to the pasture where it was quieter and more peaceful. There they sat down on a couple of tree stumps and Caroline began her lesson:

"Seven times one is seven," she began.

But it was not really the tables of seven that Caroline wished to talk about to Brother Carpenter. She stopped to think.

"Go on," said the preacher. "Seven times two is what?"

While he was waiting for her answer they could

hear the sounds of the Walker family quarreling. They had very loud, ringing voices.

"I don't think it will do the Walkers any good to go to school," she said. "And I don't think they will ever be good pioneers."

Brother Carpenter scolded her gently.

"You must not give up so soon on them. We must all try to encourage them. Once you really become friends with them, you may find they are fine people!"

The old cow, Honeysuckle, came up and stood close to Caroline. She was a rather ugly cow with crooked horns and wild-looking eyes who had come with the family on their trip from New York. Back in New York Caroline had been afraid of her and thought she was very mean.

But Caroline and the old cow had become dear friends and now Honeysuckle would follow Caroline around like a dog.

Caroline gently patted Honeysuckle's head and Brother Carpenter rubbed her shoulder.

"Think how you once disliked this good old cow," he reminded Caroline. "You even called her the Old Witch, remember?"

Caroline nodded her head and laughed.

"I think it will be harder to like the Walker family, though," she said. "At least Honeysuckle is helpful. Even when she was the mean Old Witch she gave lots of good rich milk."

"You must try," repeated Brother Carpenter.

Caroline sighed and promised to try harder to like the Walkers.

"Begin again with the sevens," said Brother Carpenter. "Try hard to get every one right."

Caroline began again:

"Seven times one is seven. Seven times one is seven. Seven words make a promise."

"What did you really want to tell me, Caroline?" asked the preacher in a patient tone. "I know it is not the tables of seven."

So Caroline told him what had happened that morning in school and how she had spoken up and told her goal in life. That was why the number seven had suddenly become so important to her.

"I am going to be a doctor," she said, counting the seven little words off on her fingers. "Those are the words I said out loud this morning in front of the whole school. 'I am going to be a doctor.' "

Brother Carpenter did not laugh.

"You have very gentle hands," he said. "I have often noticed that when you are caring for little animals or tieing up a cut, or holding a baby."

"Everybody laughed," said Caroline gloomily. "The boys were cross with me. But I want to be a doctor. Do you think that is a good goal for me?"

The young preacher thought for a while.

"When I was young I wanted to be an opera singer," he said at last. "I had a loud voice and I loved to sing. I was sure I could be a splendid opera singer."

"Why did you change your goal?" asked Caroline.

"Other people changed it for me," said the preacher. "My voice was loud enough but not sweet enough, they said. It was not right for the opera. Some people laughed when I sang. Others ran."

"That was a mean thing to do," exclaimed Caroline angrily. "I know I would have liked hearing you sing in the opera. Aren't you angry at those people?"

"Oh no," answered Brother Carpenter. "Wanting to be an opera singer has helped me to be a good preacher. I can sing in church. I can sing for the sick if I remember to sing softly. I can sing at funerals and house-raisings. I enjoy my own singing and can sing as loud as I like while I ride through the woods. Also, I think my singing helps to scare away the wild animals which might attack me if they were starving."

"When you come riding through the woods singing in your loud voice everybody cheers up," said Caroline. "No matter how downhearted they were, they cheer up. Even the worst headaches and stomach-aches are helped."

"I sing every chance I get," said the preacher. "And the more I sing the more I enjoy it. I never refuse a chance to sing."

Caroline thought for a while, stroking old Honeysuckle's smooth cheek.

"I was very lucky that those sick, mean, dirty little twins came to our house," she said at last.

"Yes, indeed," agreed the preacher. "And it was those seven little words of your goal that made you keep on trying. I saw how you wanted to give up."

He did not give Caroline time to feel proud of herself.

"You must try harder with Horace and Lewis and Dorcas and Lydia," he said. "You must coax them to go to school. School may give them a goal in life."

"I will try," promised Caroline. "And I will ask the boys to try. And my mother and father will try, too."

The rest of the family agreed, and all of them invited the Walkers to stay with them for a while and allow the four older ones to go to school with the boys and Caroline.

"Perhaps Mr. Nicholson can help give them a goal in life," said Uncle Steven hopefully.

"And when the girls see how pretty Josiebell Jones looks with her clean pink cheeks and her long curly hair and her beautiful calico dresses all ruffles and bows and buttons, they will want to wash their own hair and sew up their clothes," added Caroline. Josiebell was sixteen and the prettiest girl in school.

Things did not work out that way, however. The Walkers were not interested in goals or education or spelling. The girls only looked angry when they saw Josiebell wearing her new yellow calico with the black rosebuds.

"Back in Ohio we wore *silk* dresses and ate with

silver spoons," said Lydia as they walked home the first day.

"We rode fine horses much better than your colt Firecracker or that preacher's black horse," Horace boasted.

Always the Walker stories ended in the same way. Sile Doty, the terrible horse thief, had robbed them of horses, guns, silver spoons, and even their silk dresses.

"So that is why we are leaving Michigan and going back to Ohio," they explained. "We want a better place to live."

Steven tried to explain that if enough families lived in Pigeon County they would have a school where Latin and Greek and grammar were taught.

"Then perhaps you could study law and help make this a safer place to live," he told the Walkers.

"We ain't interested in the laws of Michigan," answered Lewis, "because we don't aim to stay around here any longer than we have to."

"We don't like your school either," said Dorcas. "We don't like that dressed-up, stuck-up blacksmith's daughter."

"What is your goal in life?" asked Caroline as

politely as she could, for it was hard to be polite to the Walkers.

"That means, what do you intend to be when you are grown up?" explained John.

"Maybe you have no goal in life yet," suggested Henry.

"Of course I do," answered Lewis angrily. "I intend to be a rich and famous burglar like Sile Doty. I mean to have a thousand horses, a million dollars, fifty pair of leather boots with long silver spurs on them, and a whole warehouse full of guns and swords and pistols."

Horace added:

"Sile Doty will be our hired man. He is the best horse thief and burglar in Michigan. Everybody is afraid of Sile Doty, even his own mother and children. But he will be *our* hired man."

"We will wear silk dresses for everyday," added Dorcas. "We will not wear calico or linsey-woolsey like you and that blacksmith's girl."

"My mother has silk dresses," cried Caroline. "And I have some which my grandfather back in New York sent me. They were too little and I never wore them."

The Walker girls tossed their heads as if they did not believe Caroline.

"We will wear silk dresses when we are grown up," declared Dorcas. "We will be married to rich burglars like Sile Doty and we will dress in silk dresses every day, not just brag about them."

"Do not lose your temper, Caroline," Steven whispered. "You look like a teakettle about to boil over!"

Caroline held her tongue between her teeth.

"Patience, patience, Caroline," she thought. "A doctor meets many wild-talking people."

But Uncle Robert spoke up for his niece.

"It would be silly to wear silk dresses for every-day," he said. "Silk dresses are for special times like weddings and funerals and parties."

"Dorcas and I will wear silk dresses every day," Lydia insisted. "Even while we cook and scrub we will wear silk dresses."

When Caroline got home she asked her mother if she might show the Walker girls the clothes which were stored away in the tin trunk under her mother's bed.

"I suppose so, if you think it would make them

feel more cheerful," agreed Mrs. Gray. "For they are surely the most downhearted girls I ever saw."

Caroline did not tell her mother her real reason for wanting to show the clothes. Her real reason was to prove to these girls that she had not just been bragging.

"Come with me," she said to the Walker girls Saturday morning. She led the girls to the bedroom and pulled the tin trunk out from under the bed.

"You see?" she said. "I was not just making it up about our silk dresses."

She showed them the scarlet taffeta and the green satin dresses which her mother had brought from New York. There were also the two pretty outfits which Grandfather Gray had sent for her birthday a couple of years ago. They were far too small and she had never worn them.

She showed them her father's wedding suit, which was still elegant though there was a moth hole in one leg.

Also there were a few ragged places in the scarlet taffeta, for a mouse had somehow managed to chew it the first year in Michigan.

All the same, the Walker girls were impressed.

They admired the clothes, smoothing the bright silks with their rough fingers.

After that they really were more cheerful. The whole family seemed to feel better, and the twins got over their sickness.

Caroline had made corncob dolls for the twins, dressing them up in pretty calico scraps. She was pleased to see how the whines of the small children had changed to laughs as they played with their dolls.

"When I am a doctor I intend to give dolls to all the sick children," she told her mother. "Dolls sometimes do more good than medicine."

"Yes, a merry heart doeth good like medicine," Mrs. Gray reminded her. "That is what my father, the doctor, often said."

Caroline nodded her head.

"Looking at pretty clothes doeth good like medicine, also," she remarked. Even Dorcas and Lydia smiled now and then.

Still the family would not be persuaded to go back to the marsh homestead and try again.

"That marsh was full of spooks," Mrs. Walker said. "You could hear them groaning day and night. In the dark you could see them walking around on the marsh."

"Many a time we have looked out at night and seen the spooks walking around carrying green fire in their hands," added Lydia.

The two girls talked a great deal about the spooks in the marsh. The things they told were very scary, and yet they were interesting, too.

"Did you ever speak to a spook?" Caroline asked one day as they walked to school.

"A person who speaks to a spook falls dead instantly," answered Dorcas.

"Or else the person is grabbed by the spook and pulled down the bottomless pool to spookland and shut up in spookland forever," added Lydia.

David shivered but wanted to hear more. "What is it like in spookland?" he asked.

"Try speaking to a spook once and you will soon find out," the Walker girls told him.

Caroline and her uncles talked about all this as they did their evening milking.

"You see why you could not be a doctor," said Robert. "Sick people live everywhere, especially by the marshes. Just suppose you had to go away back there to the marsh to see a sick person? Suppose a spook came out of the marsh and got you?"

"Being a doctor is no job for a girl," said Henry. "A man like your father or Brother Carpenter would know what to do about a spook. The spooks would quickly catch a girl."

"I have said what I have said," Caroline declared, milking away on her cow. "I have said I would be a doctor. I mean to keep my promise!"

She squeezed and pulled so hard that the old cow

gave her a cross look and switched her tail across Caroline's nose.

Uncle Henry grinned at her in a teasing way. Caroline knew what he was thinking and she knew he was right.

"Speaking up and saying things can get you into trouble. It is easier to say words than to stick to your words!"

"But anyhow," she finished, as she and the boys carried their milk pails into the house, "I don't really believe in spooks. I think the Walkers made them up. And I wouldn't be surprised if they made up Sile Doty, too!"

All in all the Grays were not sorry when the Walker family loaded back into their tumbledown wagon and rumbled off behind their slow oxen. Mrs. Gray gave them gifts of bread, cornmeal, dried apples, dried beans, ham, and a big hunk of good homemade soap.

"Good luck, good luck!" cried all the family to their departing company. The Walkers did not even so much as say "thank you"!

"A DOCTOR NEEDS
TO BE BRAVE"

5. Poor Mr. Nicholson

FOR A couple of days Caroline and all the boys had to stay home from school helping to clean house. The Walkers had left mud tracks, molasses stains, and dozens of fleas behind them.

"Brother Carpenter will be disappointed that we could not keep them in Pigeon County," said Caroline, scrubbing away. "But I am rather glad they decided to leave."

"All the same, they did know lots of scary exciting things," returned Henry, bringing another pot of boiling hot water from the fireplace.

David scoured molasses from the fireplace bench.

"All I hope is that when Caroline is a woman doctor she will never have to go down to the marshes and give medicine to children that bite like snapping turtles," he said. "If I had not been here to help you that first day, you would no doubt have given up and run."

Caroline's eyes opened wide and she felt her cheeks growing warm. But she held the end of her tongue between her teeth.

"Watch your words, Caroline!" she said to herself. "And remember that a doctor must have patience no matter how mad she feels!"

In a few days Brother Carpenter stopped to say hello. He seemed sorry that the Walkers had really gone but had cheerful news.

"A new family has taken the homestead down by the marshes," he told the Grays. "They are a young family with three little children. They will be thankful for kind neighbors good at nursing!"

"Caroline will be glad to hear that!" said Uncle John, grinning. "Caroline just loves to take care of sick sheep!"

Mr. Nicholson had stopped talking about goals now at school. Every pupil in school had told his or her goal, even the small boys of five and six, and also the girls. Most of the girls had easy goals, such as going to live in the city or taking a trip in the steamboat or having lots of fine clothes. No other girl wanted to be a doctor or a preacher or even a schoolteacher.

When he had come to the end of goals, Mr. Nicholson began on the future. He was greatly interested in the future. He was especially interested in steam trains.

For several days now they had talked about steam trains every morning. The more Mr. Nicholson talked the more excited he became.

"The time is soon coming when we will have steam trains running all over this country and railroads built through the thickest woods," he declared.

"Horses are better for travel," said Josiebell Jones, the blacksmith's daughter. "They are safer. They will go where you tell them."

"Horses are too slow for the future," declared Mr. Nicholson. "They are not strong enough. In the future I expect to see trains going past this very schoolhouse, pulling heavy loads and moving at thirty-five miles an hour!"

The pupils told of Mr. Nicholson's ideas at home. Some of the parents did not like to hear such talk.

"Thirty-five miles an hour! Why that would blow your head off!" said one girl's grandmother.

Mr. Jones, the blacksmith, talked in a loud and disgusted voice. "We hire Mr. Nicholson to teach our children how to read and write and spell and fig-ure," he said. "We do not hire him to tell tall tales. He is wasting our children's time."

Then came a house-raising over at Wolf Hill. A house-raising was a big thing in the pioneer neigh-borhood. Nearly everybody went. The men laid logs for the new house. Women cooked a big dinner. The children played and had fun.

Of course Brother Carpenter went because he was needed to lead the singing after the work was done, and also to ask the blessing on the dinner. Usually he gave a sermon at a house-raising.

"Why not ask Mr. Nicholson, the teacher, to make the speech?" said Brother Carpenter. "I hear he has a fine voice and many interesting ideas!"

So Mr. Nicholson was invited to give a short speech in the evening after the work was done or while the people were resting after dinner.

Mr. Nicholson said he would be glad to make a speech while the people rested after the big dinner.

As usual, Mr. Nicholson became rather excited when he began to speak. He got interested in talking about the future. He began telling about the railroads that would run near Wolf Hill.

As he spoke, his greenish-brownish eyes flashed. His deep, strong voice became louder and deeper and stronger.

"I expect to see trains traveling by here at thirty-five miles an hour!" he roared. "Or even forty miles an hour!"

Firecracker, the red colt who was tied to a tree nearby, suddenly snorted and tossed his head. He gave a loud whinny and stamped his foot on the ground.

Firecracker often acted this way when he got tired of standing still. But now it sounded as if he were making fun of Mr. Nicholson.

Then the blacksmith's mule joined in with a voice even louder than Mr. Nicholson's.

"Hee-haw! Hee-haw! Hee-haw!" he brayed from the bottom of his lungs. He was a stupid mule and had a habit of braying whenever another animal made any noise. He even brayed when the rooster crowed in the morning.

He tossed back his head and all his great big teeth showed in a loud laugh.

Mr. Nicholson looked at him and cried in his loudest voice:

"I expect to see trains traveling fifty miles an hour!"

Then everybody laughed. Men laughed. Women laughed. Girls laughed till tears ran down their cheeks. Boys rolled on the ground laughing. Even the babies laughed because everybody else was laughing.

Firecracker kept tossing his head and snorting and the old mule kept on hee-hawing!

Mr. Nicholson folded his arms and looked out at everybody. He waited for them to stop laughing.

Then he said, "And I expect to *ride* on that train going fifty miles an hour!"

"Poor Mr. Nicholson!" thought Caroline. "It is mean for the people to make fun of him."

She would not laugh, even though she thought Firecracker's trick was cute and funny and the old mule was silly enough to make anybody laugh.

"It is not fun to be laughed at," she thought, remembering how the scholars had all laughed when she told her goal in life. "Lots of people change their goals in life if others make fun of them."

Mr. Nicholson just stood there looking stern until the people got done laughing.

"Some people get even more determined when they are laughed at," thought Caroline. "The more people laugh, the more determined some people get."

She held her head high and tried to look stern just as Mr. Nicholson was looking.

"You and I do not give up our goals just because people laugh at us," she said to Mr. Nicholson. She said it silently, however.

The boys talked about Mr. Nicholson as they walked to school the next day. "He is a good man but a little crackbrained," said Henry.

"I wonder what crazy idea he will have today?" said John.

This morning Mr. Nicholson looked very serious. He stood in the front of the schoolroom with his arms folded across his rather ragged old coat. His greenish-brownish eyes were very stern and steady. All the scholars got so quiet that they could hear a wood beetle moving around under the bark of a log.

Then Mr. Nicholson spoke:

"I am going to leave the Pigeon Roost School," he said.

A sort of groaning sound went around the room. Everybody liked Mr. Nicholson as a teacher in spite of his crazy ideas.

"This will be my last day as your teacher," Mr. Nicholson went on.

Josiebell Jones began to sob. Caroline felt disappointed. Mr. Nicholson had looked brave that day at the house-raising. He had spoken up and he had not stopped when everybody and the horses laughed at him.

"Why are you going to quit, Mr. Nicholson?" asked Caroline. "Is it because everybody laughed at you?"

Caroline was surprised at the sound of her own voice saying her thoughts out loud.

Her uncles looked at her, frowning because nobody else had spoken and she was a girl and she had spoken up.

Mr. Nicholson looked at her hard. Then he answered her in a patient tone.

"I am not quitting, Caroline," he said. "I am not running *from,* I am running *to.* I am going to work on the railroad. I am going to help build that steam train that will run forty miles an hour!"

He told them all a little more about the new railway where he was going to work. It would be hard work, much harder than teaching school.

Finally he spoke once more to Caroline.

"In years to come when you are a grown-up woman doctor, I may see you riding one of my fast trains, going fifty miles an hour. Who knows? I may even be the engineer on that fast train. I may point you out and say, 'There goes the famous woman doctor, name's Caroline Gray. People send for her from a hundred miles away. And I was once her schoolteacher!' "

Caroline could hardly get her mind on lessons the rest of that day. She felt excited and brave. She felt she was not afraid of anything, not of snakes in the road or spooks in the marsh or even of the wicked horse thief Sile Doty himself.

She had never before realized how big and brave and handsome Mr. Nicholson really was. She felt he was a great and noble hero, almost as great as Brother Carpenter.

6. Wanted, Sile Doty!

Mr. Nicholson kept his word about going away, so all the Pigeon Roost scholars had an early vacation and a little more time at home.

"I think we ought to do something for the Merrills," said Caroline's mother one day. The Merrills were the new family who lived at the homestead by the marshes. "I think we should go visit them!"

"A good idea!" agreed Mr. Gray. "We want them to feel that this is a friendly neighborhood. Maybe you and Caroline and one of the boys would like to go today."

All the boys spoke up and told of the jobs they needed to do around home. Caroline thought it would be nice to ask the Merrills to come and visit for a few days.

"Henry could ride down and invite them," she said. "Maybe Steven would even allow him to ride on Firecracker!"

Of course she didn't believe the Walkers' stories about the spooks in the marsh, but all the same she would rather stay away from the gloomy, dangerous-looking swamp.

"I would be glad to help with all the extra work if the Merrills came to visit *us*," she pleaded.

"No, we want to help them enjoy their home," insisted Caroline's mother. "We will have a sewing bee. All the ladies around here can come. They can bring big baskets of dinner and spend the day in sewing and visiting. Sewing and visiting and eating always make women feel at home."

Caroline had never liked quilting parties. Sitting in a room where so many ladies were sewing and talking had never seemed interesting to her.

"Will I have to stay in the house and sew on

quilts?" she asked her mother. "Or may I stay outside and see that the horses do not get loose?"

"Robert can go along to look after the horses," answered Mrs. Gray. "But you will be a great help in looking after the babies and small children."

She handed Caroline a big basket of beans dried in the pods.

"You and David may shell out these beans, which I will bake for the sewing bee," she said. "While you do that, I will write the invitation for the bee."

David grumbled, "Woman's work!" and Caroline sighed as they sat down on a bench with the bean basket between them.

"Beans and babies," she sighed, "dishes and diapers. Why are all the dull jobs for girls?"

"Because those are women's jobs," David told her, opening up a dried bean pod. "They always have been; they always will be."

"Not for me," Caroline said firmly. "When I am a woman and a doctor like Grandfather Howard I shall never wash dishes. Nor shall I ever take care of a baby except to give it some medicine."

Mrs. Gray wrote out the invitation carefully in

her nicest writing and said that Caroline and the three younger uncles could ride to the Wolverene Hotel and put it up on the wall with the other notices where everybody could see it.

"Stop at every house along the way and invite the people to come," she added.

"Goody, goody!" cried David, so happy that he jumped up and spilled the basket of beans. David just loved to go to the village, and especially to the Wolverene Hotel. "When can we start?"

"As soon as you have picked up all those beans from the floor and finished shelling them," answered his sister-in-law.

Caroline and David rode double on old Dolly and Robert rode double with Henry on old Molly. The trip was fun because they had to stop along the way wherever there was a house, so they had several visits.

At the hotel, the hotelkeeper gladly agreed to put up the invitation where everybody would notice it and the hotelkeeper's wife promised to bring a basket filled with her best cooking.

It was always interesting to read the notices in the hotel and see what was going on in the community.

"A teacher is wanted for the Pigeon Roost School," Caroline read aloud.

Henry grinned. "I hope they never find one. I like it this way. No more study, no more books, no more teacher's cross old looks!"

Caroline was about to tell him he ought to be ashamed of himself when all of a sudden her glance fell on another notice:

WANTED!

SILE DOTY, MOST NOTED THIEF AND DARING
BURGLAR ALIVE. THE TERROR OF MEXICO!
LEADER OF GANG OF HORSE THIEVES,
CATTLE ROBBERS, AND HOUSEBREAKERS!

There was a good deal more about this great criminal, but Caroline did not read it all. It was enough just to know that there really *was* a robber named Sile Doty.

"Then he was real!" murmured Caroline, feeling a cold chill go down her back. "The Walkers didn't just make him up!"

The boys looked at the picture of Sile Doty. He looked more like a nice old schoolteacher than a dangerous robber. He wore a neat little black bow tie and his hair looked as if he had combed it down with goose grease.

Henry finished tacking up the invitation and read the notice about Sile Doty to the last word.

"I'm not a-scared of him," he said. "It says here he went to Mexico. I bet the Walkers never even saw him."

"But you don't know for sure," answered Caroline. With the Walkers it was hard to tell what was real and what was make-believe.

"If Sile Doty is real then maybe spooks are real, too," she said to David as she and her youngest uncle went out of the hotel. "Do you suppose there really might be spooks in the marsh?"

"I don't even want to know," answered David. "I'm not afraid of the spooks when I'm with a lot of other people, like at the sewing bee. But I wouldn't want to be fooling around a marsh by myself and I wouldn't want to live there, either!"

A rather gloomy thought came to Caroline.

"If that new family down by the marsh should get sick we would have to go and help them," she said. "Brother Carpenter would expect Mother to go and Mother would expect me to go with her."

"You wouldn't be much of a doctor if you were afraid to visit the sick because they lived by a marsh," said David sensibly. "Sick people need doctors even if there are spooks behind their house."

"You are right," Caroline told him. "I intend to do my best to see that the Merrills stay healthy."

She stopped at the medicine store and spent all her money on a great big bottle of health tonic.

The printing on the bottle said that the tonic would keep away chills, fever, boils, toothache, headache, earache, and itch.

"This will be a good present for the Merrill family," she told David, who was spending his money on sour balls and peppermint sticks.

"I don't think they'll like it," declared David. "If you want to give them something useful, why don't you give them one of those steel traps? They could set it down by the marsh and catch every spook that showed up."

"I want the Merrills to stay strong and healthy," mumbled Caroline, chewing on a sour ball which the medicine man gave her. "If they stay strong and healthy, they can catch their own spooks."

7. "Caroline Gray won't run away"

THE QUILTING bee was a great success and it was certainly more exciting than most parties where only women and children went.

Early in the morning Mrs. Gray, Caroline, and the three youngest uncles set off toward the marshes driving Molly and Dolly hitched to the small wagon.

Though this was a ladies' party and Henry was twelve years old, he felt he should go along to protect the ladies from such dangers as Indians, burglars, or wild animals which had escaped from shows.

Robert knew he would be needed to help care for

the horses. And David was considered a baby by the rest of the family, so of course he was invited with the ladies.

The small wagon was well loaded with gifts for the Merrills, the well-filled dinner baskets, and Henry's gun, which Grandfather Gray had given him as a going-away gift three years ago.

Caroline carried the large bottle of medicine carefully. She hoped the Merrill family would begin taking it that very day.

As they went by the long stretch of marsh the children looked closely. It was a dreary place with dead trees sticking up through the still, stagnant water. Frogs bellowed from the bog, and ugly-looking birds sat perched on the leafless trees.

But they saw no spooks.

"Spooks are not real, anyhow!" said Caroline bravely.

"All the same a marsh is a dangerous place and you stay away from it," said Henry bossily. "A person could get stuck in that marsh mud and starve to death!"

He reached into one of the baskets and took out a raw potato, which he peeled and ate with a loud crunching sound.

"Starving to death is a terrible way to die!" he remarked.

The Grays were the first to arrive, but soon many others began to come and everybody was busy. The ladies made extra tables of boards laid across logs, put out their baskets, and hung kettles of soup and other food over the fireplace.

Henry and Robert found hitching places for the horses while Caroline and David played with the small children.

Of course Brother Carpenter was there. No big gathering would be complete without him. He was good-looking and strong and cheerful and all the women liked his singing.

Besides he could cook, lift heavy things, take care of the sick, and settle quarrels.

The marsh homestead was beginning to look better by this time. Mrs. Merrill worked hard to keep the house clean and Mr. Merrill worked even harder repairing the barn, building a new woodshed, and providing food.

Today the house was so crowded that there was hardly enough room. They really needed an extra house just for the babies and children.

"What about the new woodshed?" said Caroline. The woodshed had no roof, but it was not raining anyway. It was a nice great big sort of pen made of rough logs which had a pleasant woodsy smell.

The ground was soft with grass and moss and there were some wild honeysuckle vines growing down at one end which gave a lovely perfume all around.

"And when dinner is over and the babies get sleepy for their naps, we can spread blankets on the ground and they can sleep right here in the shed."

"You have such bright ideas, Caroline," praised Josiebell. She was looking very pretty today in a yellow calico dress with many ruffles and bows. And she added, "Of course some of your ideas are silly, but you will get over wanting to be a woman doctor."

"A doctor's life is very dangerous," said the hotel-keeper's wife, taking a big meat pie from her basket. "Let women do safe things like caring for the babies and cooking good meals and let the men be doctors, I say!"

The forenoon went by very pleasantly. The dinner was magnificent with everything good to eat and as much cake as anybody wanted. The small children ate their dinner in the shed with Caroline and some of the younger girls helping to feed them.

"Still, I am getting just a little tired of all these babies and small children," said the mill owner's daughter. She wanted to go in and stay with the big girls and listen to their interesting talk.

When the babies began to get sleepy and were bedded down for their naps, the other girls went off to walk and tell secrets.

Some quite old grandmothers who also got sleepy came out with their knitting. They sat on a big log at one end of the shed and leaned against the wall. They knitted and nodded and chatted. They yawned and took little catnaps.

"Come on, Caroline," one of the girls called, looking through a crack in the shed. "We're going to talk secrets. The babies are all right. Come on."

A couple of the babies were cranky and would not go to sleep. One wanted to pick weeds and eat them. One got a stomachache and cried. One wanted his mother.

"Grandma will look after the babies," said a girl who lived over by Wolf Creek. "She looks after our babies all day long."

"Then she is likely tired of it too," answered Caroline sensibly. There was no way out of it. She would have to stay in here till all the babies went to sleep, no matter how tired she got of it. Would a good woman doctor go off and leave a house full of dying people just because she wanted to talk secrets?

The answer was no. Being a doctor often got monotonous.

One of the grandmothers looked up from her nodding and knitting to praise Caroline.

"You are a good hand with the babies. Your mother is good with the sick, too. You are going to be just like her, when you are her age."

Caroline smiled, as she patted the baby and got ready to lay him down in a sweet-smelling corner shaded by the honeysuckle.

"When I am my mother's age I am going to be doing something more important and more exciting than taking care of babies at a quilting bee," she said. But she said it to herself this time.

Just as she got the baby nicely settled on the ground, she got the worst scare of her life.

Not more than a foot away from the baby was a great big copperhead snake stretched out below the vines!

Now a copperhead snake is not like a harmless black snake. A copperhead is mean and its bite is deadly poison. Caroline had never met a copperhead eye to eye before and for a minute she wondered if she might be having a bad dream.

Her father had once told her, "When you see a snake with an ax-shaped head just the color of your little cooking kettle, you must get out of the way quickly. Never argue with a copperhead!"

Caroline wished to turn and run. She felt like screaming for help. And she knew that she must not run and she must not scream. It was up to her to kill the snake.

She looked all around while the old grandmothers gossiped and knit up at the other end of the shed, and some of the children laughed and played. She held her tongue between her teeth to keep from yelling, which would scare the babies and give the snake a good excuse to bite one of them.

Then she saw that luck was really with her. Somebody had left a big piece of wood on the ground. It was a thick, heavy piece with the ends sharpened where it had been cut. It was just right for killing a snake if you were sure and steady and took good aim to bring the wood down exactly in the right place on that bright copper triangle.

Caroline took careful aim with the log of wood and brought it down hard in just the right place.

Trembling, and yet feeling very triumphant, Caroline suddenly remembered that her father had also told her that where you found one copperhead you found two, for they traveled in pairs.

In less than a minute she saw the other one, even

bigger and brighter than its mate. Once again she aimed with her piece of wood and once again she brought it down with all her might and once again she hit exactly the right place.

The whimpering baby had gone back to sleep and the grandmothers were talking and laughing over their knitting. The children up at the other end were still playing with their corncob dolls just as if Caroline had not just lived through the most dangerous adventure of her life.

She was trembling all over and her face felt cold and she answered rather breathlessly when one of the grandmothers looked at her and asked if she was sick.

"No, I'm not sick," she said. "But I've just killed two snakes, two copperhead snakes. I've killed two snakes all by myself. You don't believe me, do you?"

"Lots of snakes around this time of year," said one of the grandmothers yawning. "They get to be a real nuisance sometimes."

"But these were *copperhead* snakes," said Caroline. "I killed them, two of them. Two copperhead snakes and *I* killed them."

Another grandmother said, "The copperhead is a

mean snake. But you're lucky it wasn't rattlesnakes. A rattlesnake really fights!"

The grandmothers did not seem greatly impressed. They did not realize what a tremendous thing it was for Caroline to kill two copperhead snakes.

But a little later Caroline went back and hunted up Uncle Henry and Uncle David and Uncle Robert. She made them come with her to the shed and look at the dead snakes.

"And I killed them," she said. "I killed them because I did not want them to bite the Hineline baby."

The boys looked at her in silence. They would not have believed her except that Caroline never told lies.

"So you see what I would do if a snake got in my way when I started out to see a sick person?" she said.

"But what if they would bite you first, Caroline?" said David. He was about to cry so he spoke in a very angry tone. "If a snake bit you and you died, who would help me with the milking? Who would stir the apple butter? Who would set the table and help with the dishes?"

Uncle Henry scolded a little, too.

"You should stay away from copperhead snakes, Caroline. If a copperhead bites you, how are you going to grow up and be a doctor? And who would help with the cooking?"

But Robert did not scold. He simply stared first at Caroline and then at the snakes and could hardly find any words strong enough to express his feelings. "Yellow-bellied sapsuckers!" he kept muttering.

Finally he managed to say something else.

"Just wait till Brother Carpenter hears about this! He will hardly believe it. He'll never believe it!"

As they rode home that evening Uncle David moved up close to Caroline in the wagon.

"I have changed that poem I wrote about you," he told her. "You remember the one that said, 'Dr. Gray, run away, because a snake is in your way'?"

Caroline nodded. She remembered.

"This is the way it goes now," said David. He recited rather loudly:

"Caroline Gray, won't run away,
    Even if copperheads get in the way!"

Caroline said she thought the poem was as beautiful as anything in the whole shelf of books at school.

"All the same, you stay away from copperheads!" commanded Robert angrily. "Who would look after our hornet stings and cuts and thorns in our feet if a copperhead made you die!"

8. A gift from the boys

FOR SEVERAL days Caroline's great battle with the copperheads was the favorite subject for conversation.

Mrs. Gray turned pale as she listened to the story on the way home from the quilting bee. The boys described the snakes to her and made them sound more like dragons than plain old copperheads.

Though she turned pale she was proud of her daughter.

"All our relatives back in New York will want to hear about this," she said proudly.

Mr. Gray laughed when he heard about the snakes. "I do wish I could have seen that fight!"

he said. "It took a brave girl to kill those copper-heads."

"Especially when the girl was Caroline, who just hates to kill anything," added Steven. Caroline would not even kill a mouse and she was always taking care of hurt birds, orphan lambs, and so forth.

So for two or three days Caroline really felt important in the family. Steven wrote a letter to Grandfather Gray telling all the news and describing Caroline's brave fight.

Mrs. Gray wrote a letter to her parents, Grandfather and Grandmother Howard. She told them all the news and described Caroline's adventure. Caroline herself added a couple of lines to the letter in her best writing.

"I have decided to be a doctor when I grow up," she wrote. She wondered what Grandfather Howard would think about women doctors. She hoped he would approve, but even if he did not approve, she intended to keep her word.

Steven had even allowed her to take several rides on Firecracker, which he considered the greatest favor he could give anybody.

But after about ten days the boys began to go

back to their old ways and treat Caroline like just a girl instead of a heroine.

One Saturday, for instance, the five of them went over to the village.

"Let me go too," begged Caroline. It was fun to go to the village. You could never tell what pretty new things might be in the store or what exciting notices on the wall at the hotel.

But the boys absolutely and flatly refused even though Caroline offered to ride double with David on old Dolly.

"This is a men's trip. We do not want any girls along," said Uncle David.

"Everybody knows how scairdy girls are on a trip!" declared Uncle John with a big wink which made him look like a clown.

"Besides," added Henry, "today is my birthday in case you have forgotten and I would like to have a fine supper with one of your maple molasses hickory nut cakes."

"A girl's place is really at home anyhow, helping with the cooking and washing," added Robert.

The boys really seemed to be trying to make Caroline angry and they were succeeding, too. Caroline felt her temper boiling like a teakettle and she wanted to throw a dish of apple butter right into their grinning faces.

But she bit her lips and held her peace.

"Be patient, Caroline, be patient!" she told herself. "Remember that a doctor meets many stupid men in her work."

When the boys had disappeared into the woods road, Caroline washed her face and hands, brushed her black hair, put a bit of wheat flour on her nose to cover up the freckles, and dressed in her new pink calico.

She got the book of fairy tales which had been last year's Christmas present from her prettiest aunt back in New York and sat down by the window to read.

"If I am going to be treated like a girl, then I intend to act like a lady," she told her mother. "I shall not do any work today, especially not any cooking to make my dress sticky and my hands smoky."

"You must make up your own mind," said her mother. She filled the soup kettle with meat and dried beans. "Soup is easy to cook and is very nourishing, even for a birthday dinner."

Mr. Gray was surprised, when he came into the house, to see his dressed-up daughter.

"How beautiful you look!" he exclaimed. "You seem dressed to go some place. I am going over to Grayling to the court meeting. Would you like to go?"

Grayling was another town in a different direction from Pigeon Roost. It was a little town but it had a good store and a hotel where interesting travelers often stopped.

"You look pretty enough to go any place," said her father. "We will not get back tonight, of course, but the hotelkeeper's children would love to have company."

"Shall I go?" Caroline asked her mother.

"You must make up your own mind," answered her mother. "I cannot go because my bread must be baked this afternoon. But go if you wish. The boys will be back to keep me company."

"It will be good enough for them," thought Caroline, still feeling angry. "They will be sorry when they know I went to Grayling while they were only at Pigeon Roost."

She thought of this evening when the boys would

come back home. She would not be here. There would be no maple molasses hickory nut cake.

Henry, who loved to eat, and who specially loved Caroline's maple molasses hickory nut cake, would be really disappointed. It would serve him right, too!

She kissed her mother good-by and went with her father out to where his gray riding horse stood waiting. The horse looked at her in amazement and stamped one foot.

"Even old Snort is proud to carry such a dressed-up young lady," her father said. "All you need to look like a real lady is a pretty purse to carry." Caroline was carrying her night things tied up in a square of calico.

Caroline jumped up onto old Snort's back with her father's help. Off they galloped. But after going a very short distance, Caroline said:

"Please stop. I have decided not to go after all. I must go back."

"Your mother will be all right," said Mr. Gray. "The boys will be home before dark."

"I must go back," said Caroline. So her father stopped the horse and helped her off.

"A woman has a right to change her mind, I suppose," he said. "Though I wish all those men at the meeting could see what a pretty daughter I have."

"Good-by, Father," called Caroline. "When you get home tomorrow I will have a nice cake baked for you."

She stepped into a mud puddle as she was running back, and her Sunday slippers and new dress got rather splashed. A green garter snake lay in her way but she merely jumped over him.

Her mother was amazed when she came back into the kitchen, muddy and breathless.

"What happened to the fine lady who was going to the meeting?" she cried.

"I am not really a fine lady, I guess," sighed Caroline. "I am just the girl in the family."

"You and I can have a good time today, just us girls," said her mother. "We will work on our samplers, talk secrets, and maybe curl our hair."

"And while you are baking the bread I would like to bake a maple molasses hickory nut cake if I may," said Caroline.

She went into her room and took off her best

clothes, putting on her old blue dress and her brown pinafore apron.

The day went by in a very pleasant way and both Mrs. Gray's bread and Caroline's cake turned out well. The whole house had a lovely smell of fresh bread and sweet maple molasses.

Since Mrs. Gray was the best cook in Pigeon County and did not want to get out of practice she made several other good dishes.

The boys came home and rushed into the kitchen sniffing with joy at the delicious smells and looking very pleased with themselves.

They gathered around Caroline and then Uncle Henry took a package from his pocket. It was wrapped in thin blue paper and tied with gold-colored string. He handed the package to Caroline.

"It is from all of us," he said. "But it was my idea."

Inside the package was a long bag, or purse.

It was made of snakeskin, as soft and beautiful as satin. It was lined with yellow silk, and it had a black velvet drawstring decorated with seven gold buttons.

"We took those snakes you killed to the taxidermist," said John proudly. "He skinned the snakes and dried the skins and made them into this fine bag."

"We paid for the bag with our own money," said Robert, "and each of us put a coin in it."

"I put in the two-bit piece I was saving for a sack of candy," added Henry.

"This is the finest gift I have ever had," declared Caroline.

She slipped the velvet drawstring over her arm. It was just the right size and length and everything.

"It will be very useful," said Steven. "It will hold most anything you want; sewing things, clothes, money, a book, medicine—anything!"

"When you are a doctor, riding around, this bag will be a great help to you," remarked David.

"The seven buttons will keep you reminded," said Steven. "They will keep you reminded of something you said one morning in school."

THE VALUABLE
SNAKESKIN BAG

9. Danger in the marsh

CAROLINE was so proud of her snakeskin bag that she took it with her every time she went outside the house.

"It will soon get dirty and dull," her mother told her, but Caroline said:

"It is a great help to me. It makes me feel brave. It reminds me of the time the boys were proud of me. And besides it holds so many things."

She wore it over her arm when she went to church and everybody admired it.

"It is my reward for killing the copperheads,"

Caroline told everybody. "The boys gave it to me. They spent their own money for it!"

"What are the seven gold buttons for?" asked Josiebell Jones.

"That is sort of a secret," Caroline answered. Those seven little buttons said the seven little words that had started everything that morning in school.

"I think a whole string of buttons would have looked prettier," said Josiebell, "like a dozen buttons or maybe two dozen."

She looked at the long row of gold-colored buttons on her new blue dress.

"There are thirty buttons on my dress," she said proudly.

Caroline smiled but did not answer with the question which was in her mind.

"But what do you think about when you look at those thirty buttons?" she was wondering.

That Sunday Brother Carpenter had a new song which he taught the people to sing. Since he was so fond of music and singing he always spent quite a bit of time at the church meetings in singing.

"This is a fine song for pioneer people to sing,"

he declared. "If everybody does what this song says, our community will grow better and better."

He sang in a voice which was louder and sweeter than thunder, and Caroline felt he was singing especially for her.

"Go to the pillow of disease
    Where night gives no repose;
And on the cheek where sickness preys,
    Bid health to plant the rose!

"Go where the friendless stranger lies;
    To perish is his doom;
Snatch from the grave his closing eyes,
    And bring his blessing home!"

"What a beautiful, beautiful song!" the ladies murmured to one another. Josiebell Jones sang like a bird so that her father looked at her with great pride. Caroline sang with all her might.

The snakeskin bag lay silky soft in her lap. The seven buttons around the drawstring seemed to echo the beautiful words of the song.

Caroline had a thought which she kept very silent and to herself:

"When I am a woman doctor riding my black

horse Steam around to see the sick, and carrying my medicine to the pillow of disease, I shall sing this song in a loud, sweet voice just as Brother Carpenter does."

It was easy to imagine herself riding a black horse through the forest, singing as she rode along. The sick would raise their heads from their pillows of disease and would feel stronger.

"Here comes the brave woman doctor, Caroline Gray. We shall not perish after all!"

There were not many friendless strangers around the Pigeon County neighborhood because Brother Carpenter was constantly visiting everybody and trying to make them feel at home.

Still, there must be a few friendless strangers needing a kind girl to smooth their pillows and help make their cheeks rosy again.

Anyway, it was something interesting to think about as she milked cows, washed dishes, or shelled beans. She practiced singing the new hymn as she worked on these rather dull tasks.

No more than a week after she had learned the song Mr. Merrill came up from his home down by the marsh. He looked very discouraged.

All his family were sick in bed he told Mrs. Gray.

His wife was too sick to keep house. His little children cried all day.

"Even I am not feeling at all well and I sometimes wonder if I should give up trying to make a home in Michigan!" he said, drinking a cup of hot sassafras tea which Mrs. Gray gave him.

"You must not think of leaving," Mr. Gray cheered the young man. "Michigan is getting better all the time."

"Your wife needs another woman around for a few days," declared Mrs. Gray. "Your little children need a cheerful girl to play with them for a while."

"But, Mother!" cried Caroline. "Have you forgotten that Brother Carpenter is going to be teaching the Pigeon Roost School this month? I *need* to go to school!"

She looked at David and Robert, who were out in the front yard playing horseshoes.

"Take one of the boys with you," she begged. "They are big and strong. They can carry things like wood and water. They are not afraid of rats or snakes."

Mrs. Gray gave Mr. Merrill a loaf of fresh bread and promised that she and Caroline would be over very soon with medicines and other things. The pale young man looked better as he rode away.

"I hate to miss school when Brother Carpenter is the teacher," mourned Caroline. "Couldn't I go to the Merrills some other time?"

"Now is when they need us," answered her mother. She added with a smile:

"How often I remember how my father, the doctor, had to get out of bed when he wanted to sleep, or ride through the snow when he wished to sit by the bright fire. And he even missed most of my wedding dinner because he had to go look after a boy who had shot off his big toe by mistake."

"A doctor has a very hard life," remarked Steven. He felt rather sorry for Caroline. "You may ride Firecracker," he offered.

So Caroline felt quite cheerful as she and her mother rode off early Monday morning. The snakeskin bag jingled pleasantly from her arm reminding her that she had conquered in a battle with really dangerous snakes.

And riding the red colt was exciting. He pranced and jumped and snorted and stepped very high. He pretended to be afraid if a bush flipped against his nose or a rabbit jumped up in front of him, but he was really just having fun because he liked to jump and snort.

He jumped and snorted as they went past the marsh. It was a gruesome, ghostly-looking place, a great wide spread of green-black water with dead, drowned trees sticking up out of it, and thick grass and rushes at the edge.

Marsh birds pecked around among the grass and rushes with sad, sobbing cries. And as they got almost past the stretch of marsh Caroline was sure she heard a sort of a wailing cry, different from the birds' calls.

"Did you hear anything strange as we went past the marsh?" she asked her mother. "A sort of moaning like a spook?"

Mrs. Gray laughed merrily.

"An owl in a treetop makes a spooky noise," she said, "and a heron wading after a snake may also."

Caroline patted Firecracker's head. He had been looking at the swamp in a nervous way.

"Stop being scared, Firecracker!" she said. "Spooks are only make-believe."

Mr. Merrill was out in his barnyard trying to do the chores when Caroline and her mother rode up.

He looked pale and shaky and much too sick to be outdoors working. But his face brightened at the sight of the visitors.

"You are a sight for sore eyes," he said thankfully. "Already I feel better."

Caroline and her mother slid from their horses and went into the house, lugging their gifts of food, medicine, and blankets.

"You come right on in and go to bed, too," Mrs. Gray called as Mr. Merrill led the horses to the barn.

The house seemed very dreary since the fire was nearly out, there was nothing cooking in the iron pot, and everything had a dirty, neglected appearance.

Even the sounds were dreary, for the children were crying and Mrs. Merrill was coughing and shivering.

"Thank goodness for neighbors like you," she sighed. "Already I feel better."

"A merry heart doeth good like medicine," answered Mrs. Gray cheerfully. "That is what my father used to say and he is a doctor who makes medicine."

Caroline hung her snakeskin bag from a peg on

the wall and immediately got very busy. She found kindling and built up the fire while her mother hung the water kettle over the blaze and got out her bags of medicinal herbs.

By the time Mr. Merrill came in things were looking more cheerful. The fire was high and bright. Steam was coming from the kettle. There was a pleasant smell from the food Mrs. Gray had brought in the big basket.

Caroline had found the broom and was sweeping away at the mud on the floor.

"Diddle, diddle, diddle, my son John,
He went to bed with his stockings on.
Diddle, diddle, diddle, my girl Grace,
She spilled molasses all over her face!"

Grace was the Merrills' second child. She had been crying, but she stopped crying and began to smile a little.

"You are better than any medicine in the Pigeon Roost store," said Mrs. Merrill as Caroline brought her a cup of hot herb tea.

Mr. Merrill nodded his head as he drank the herb tea Mrs. Gray had made for him.

"I was ready to give up and go back to Massachusetts," he said. "But already I feel stronger and more hopeful."

Caroline washed the Merrill children's faces. She straightened up their beds and helped feed them with hot soup. They were not like the Walker twins. They smiled at her, were glad to have their faces washed, and ate their good soup eagerly.

"How long can you stay?" John asked. "Can you stay a long time?"

"We will stay until Mrs. Merrill is well enough to be up and cook again," Mrs. Gray promised.

So when Caroline awoke the fourth morning and saw that Mrs. Merrill was getting the breakfast she felt cheerful.

"We will go home today!" she thought, very happy. "We are no longer needed and we can go home!"

But she was mistaken. This morning it was Caroline's mother who was sick. She had a terrible headache. Her face was red with fever and she felt chilly.

Caroline was worried. She brought her mother a cup of hot tea to drink. She put cloths dipped in cold water on her mother's forehead.

Mrs. Gray tried to cheer up her daughter. "It is nothing but one of my headaches," she said. "If I were at home I would go to my herb cabinet and quickly cure the headache with some of my fennel blossom tea."

Caroline often went with her mother to gather herbs for medicine. She knew just how the fennel plants looked and smelled. And she remembered seeing some of their yellow flowers along the road as she and her mother came by the marsh.

"Oh, Caroline, I am thankful for your sharp eyes," sighed her mother when Caroline told her this. "If you would only go get some of the plants! Can you remember where you saw them?"

Caroline could remember exactly. She had noticed the yellow blossoms at the edge of the marsh as she was looking at the greenish pond.

So now away she ran, promising to be back very soon. She raced swiftly toward the marsh, not even paying any attention to a couple of garter snakes at the side of her path. The pennies in the snakeskin bag jingled cheerfully as she ran and helped give her courage. "A doctor must always be very brave," they jingled.

Soon she came in sight of the patch of yellow fennel. It was closer to the marsh than she had thought, and she had to be careful not to step into the soft mud.

Just as she got ready to stretch out her hand for the plants she heard a terrible, mournful howl. It sounded for all the world like a spook moaning, "No, no, no!"

Caroline drew back her hand, trembling all over, feeling cold shivers of fright.

She looked out over the marsh, half expecting to see a spook rising up out of the slimy water. She saw only the slippery greenish water with a few birds flitting around and grabbing for the mosquitoes and snake feeders which lived in the water.

She reached again and got a handful of the fennel. And once again she heard that wailing, this time louder and more dreadful than ever. It seemed to be saying, "Go-O-O-O-O-O! Go-O-O-O-O-O-O-O!"

"But first I am going to get these fennel plants!" Caroline answered the spook. She remembered that the Walker girls had said that anyone who spoke to a spook would die instantly. She waited an instant and did not die so she felt bolder.

"You do not scare me, Spook!" she called loudly. She pulled another handful of the sweet-smelling fennel.

This time the howling was even louder. It went up and down, ending on a high note which was a little bit like a wolverene's scream.

[100]

Maybe it was a wolverene! A wolverene is a very savage and dangerous animal, and a wolverene is real. Caroline pulled one last handful of the fennel blossoms and got ready to race back.

Then she saw the spook which had been howling at her. It was very close; not more than a few yards away at the edge of the marsh!

10. The rescue

"So YOU are the spook!" she said, looking closer, taking a few steps nearer.

Her spook was only a dog which had become caught in the soft mud of the marsh and was hanging over an old dead branch just as you would hang a mop rag over a fence. The branch was all that kept the dog from sinking to the bottom of the bottomless marsh.

The dog had seen her and he had been howling for help! Hardly any of him showed except his head and shoulders. She could tell he was nearly worn out and would soon become too weak to hang on to the branch.

She looked at him wondering what to do and he looked back at her with a terrible pleading and hope in his eyes.

She could not reach him without stepping into the soft, wicked marsh mud. Then her mother would never get the fennel for her headache.

"Good boy! Good dog! Hang on, I will bring help. I *promise* I will," said Caroline. The dog looked at her as if she were big and strong and wise and knew just what to do.

Caroline did *not* know what to do but she did know that if she went back to the house for help it would be too late.

"If I only had a rope!" she thought. And then her big idea came to her. She had a dress. It was rather long and it was strong. It was, at least, a chance.

She stuffed the fennel plants into the snakeskin bag and took the bag from over her arm. Then she slipped out of her dress. It was not quite long enough, but when she fastened her belt to the long sleeves it was just right.

She wrapped the leather belt around her wrists and threw the hem of the dress as far out as she could. She hoped and prayed the dog was smart enough to know what she was doing.

He knew. He seized the hem of Caroline's linsey-woolsey dress and fastened his big teeth on it. "Hold on, hold tight!" begged Caroline. "Good dog! Brave dog! Valiant dog! Come on!"

Not too fast, but steadily and with all her might, Caroline pulled. The greedy, sucking marsh mud pulled back. The dog held on for life.

And at last Caroline had him out of the marsh and on safe ground. He was too weak to walk or even to stand up, but he licked her hand. He was near death from starvation.

Caroline managed to drag him up under a tree. She left him there with her mud-soaked dress for company. She gave him a pat or two between the ears and some small bites of a sandwich which Henry had put into the bag.

"Stay here! I will be back. Stay!" she commanded. The dog seemed to understand. He laid his head on the soggy dress and did not howl as she sped back to her mother. Weakly he nibbled at the food.

Mr. Merrill saw her coming and dropped his water pail in amazement. Mrs. Merrill dropped the pot she was scouring when Caroline rushed into the house. "Your dress, Caroline, what happened?" she screamed.

Mrs. Gray sat up in bed. Caroline had forgotten how strange she must look, wearing only muddy underpants and holding the snakeskin bag in one muddy hand.

"Where is your dress, Caroline?" her mother asked.

"It is down by the marsh where I found the spook," answered Caroline. "But first, you must have your fennel blossom tea!"

While Mrs. Merrill was pouring hot water over the yellow blossoms, and Caroline was putting on one of Mrs. Merrill's dresses, Caroline told the story of the rescue.

Everyone listened in amazement, including Mr. Merrill, who had rushed into the house in wild excitement, shouting:

"What caught you, Caroline? What caught you?"

"I will go down to the marsh and get the dog," offered Mr. Merrill.

The fennel blossom tea was done by this time and Mrs. Merrill poured some into one of her prettiest cups. Caroline carried it to her mother.

"I am not even sure I need it any more," said Mrs. Gray, laughing. "Your exciting story almost made my headache go away!"

Soon Mr. Merrill came back into the house carrying the dog, who was still too weak to walk.

"Mighty near gone," said the young man cheerfully. "Two more hours and he'd've been buzzard food!"

The ladies shuddered.

"And such a beautiful dog, under all that mud and slime," said Mrs. Gray.

Caroline wiped the mud and the slithery green slime from the dog's coat. She washed him with warm water and some of her own mother's homemade soap.

Then she fed him spoonfuls of good soup, which he ate gratefully, stopping between swallows to lick her hand.

"He is certainly different from the Walker twins," laughed Caroline. And she added to herself, "Of course, a doctor meets all kinds of people with all kinds of tempers; good ones, mean ones."

Spook was going to be one of the good ones. And yet, maybe in a way, the Walkers had led her to Spook.

"I wonder whatever happened to the Walkers," said

Caroline's mother. "Those poor, unlucky people!"

Mr. Merrill looked at Spook later on. Though thin as a skeleton, he was a beautiful animal; an Irish Setter with long reddish-brownish hair and long ears, one with a little mark in it.

"He is a fine dog," said the young man. "Some emigrant has lost him. This mark on his ear shows you."

A tiny hole had been made in the end of the dog's ear, like the holes that ladies make for earrings.

"And look!" cried Caroline. "There is a little earring in it, a tiny little golden earring."

Mr. Merrill was impressed.

"That shows this dog once had an owner who was very proud of him," he said. "Only a very fine dog would be marked with a golden earring."

Caroline stroked the dog's head and he wagged his tail weakly but happily.

"You still have an owner who is very proud of you," she said to him. "And you will follow me on all my trips and we will protect each other!"

In a day or so Caroline and her mother were able to go home, Spook riding on the horse with Mrs.

Gray. Firecracker was too frisky and nervous to carry a dog on his back.

The boys listened in amazement to the story of Spook's rescue.

"Why must you have all the exciting adventures?" complained Robert. "All we got to do was go to school while you were down by the marshes having fun and meeting danger and rescuing dogs."

"Why must you be so different from most girls?" grumbled John. "Most girls have safe, quiet lives while the boys do the dangerous things."

Caroline only smiled. The trouble with the boys was that they had been compelled to eat their own cooking for several days. That always made them cross.

But they all loved the new dog and liked to have him around.

Steven carved willow whistles, which made a clear, loud call. He gave one to Caroline and kept one.

"We will teach the dog to come when he hears this whistle," said Steven. "Should danger come suddenly, you can blow this whistle and he will come running. That is better than calling, 'Spook, Spook, Spook!' "

"A dog like this deserves to be called Bonnie Prince Charlie or Napoleon or George Washington," declared John. "Spook is a silly-sounding name."

"Hero would be a fine name for him," suggested Robert. "That would give him something to live up to."

"His name is Spook," Caroline always answered these arguments. "That name gives *me* something to live up to."

"How silly you talk, just like a silly girl," Henry said in a disgusted voice one time.

Caroline only smiled. "Spook" might be a silly name, but when she said it or heard it, she would remember how scared she had been down by the marsh and she would remember that she had overcome that fear.

"And the very thing that scared me so turned out to be one of my greatest treasures and one of my truest friends. Spook is a beautiful name!"

Caroline said these words to herself, stroking

Spook's silky head. Some thoughts a girl kept to herself, away from the boys.

Spook was very faithful to Caroline. He liked the boys. He seemed proud to be part of the family. He was polite and loving to them all. But Caroline was the one he followed. Caroline was the one he sat by when the family rode in the wagon. When they all rode horseback he did not follow the prancing Firecracker or the high-stepping Snort.

He walked along behind old Dolly or fat old Molly, the safe, gentle mares who usually carried Caroline.

On Sunday he went to church with the family. He walked proudly into church, keeping close to Caroline's heels.

He was so clean and beautiful, and so well behaved in church, that nobody objected when he came inside and lay down at Caroline's feet.

"I do hope that Brother Carpenter will know about somebody who is sick and needs to be visited," Caroline had said to her mother as they rode along the woods road to Pigeon Roost. "Some rather nice person not too far back in the woods."

She held her head high just as Brother Carpenter always did, and she sang one of the songs he had taught the people.

Caroline's voice was not so loud and ringing as Brother Carpenter's, nor did old Dolly prance and snort in the manner of the preacher's horse.

But Caroline could easily imagine she was riding a fiery steed to where some friendless stranger was lying. In the bag over her arm was medicine for all kinds of diseases.

Behind her followed her faithful dog, ready to defend her from any danger.

She felt that she had made a good start toward her goal.

Brother Carpenter admired Spook very much.

"He is a young dog, too," declared the preacher, looking at Spook's big white teeth. "By the time you are a grown woman he should still be a strong, faithful companion for you."

When they sang the new hymn that morning, Caroline sang with all her heart. Though the song had always seemed beautiful to her it seemed especially beautiful now. It seemed so *true*.

"Go where the friendless stranger lies;
    To perish is his doom;
Snatch from the grave his closing eyes,
    And bring his blessing home!"

Caroline sang these lovely words at the top of her voice. Spook lay at her feet with his head on her toes.

"You are not a friendless stranger any more," Caroline whispered tenderly to him. "I have snatched you from the grave and brought you home!"

"I AM GOING AWAY FOR A VISIT"

11. Stolen treasure

"MY SUNDAY dress is getting too tight," complained Caroline one Sunday when she was putting on her best clothes to go to church. "The armholes pinch. The sleeves are too short. The bottom ruffle is almost up to my knees."

"You are growing, Caroline," answered her mother. "You need a new Sunday dress."

"May I have a silk dress?" asked Caroline. "Several of the big girls have silk dresses for Sunday. Am I old enough?"

"I have a good idea," said her mother. "I think I could cut down one of my old silk dresses for you. I have saved them for years and they are too tight for me. But they are still good."

"May I have the red one?" begged Caroline. She could imagine herself dressed in the red silk, looking very grown up and elegant.

She wanted to go that very minute and open up the tin trunk but her mother said they would wait till the next day.

"First thing in the morning we will get out the dresses," she promised.

First thing next morning Caroline hurried to the tin trunk. She opened it wide. Then she gave a loud cry of surprise and disappointment and anger.

The silk dresses were gone. The dainty little outfits that Grandfather Gray had sent for her birthday three years ago were gone.

Even Mr. Gray's wedding suit was gone. Indeed, the trunk was nearly empty. Only some bundles of old letters and the good linen tablecloths were left.

"The Walker girls took them!" cried Caroline. She was too angry to cry and she wished the Walker girls were there so she could fight with them.

"To think I saved those clothes for years and years and years," said Mrs. Gray, wiping away some tears. "They were too beautiful to give away and too fancy to wear here in Michigan, but still it was nice to have them. They were a treasure to me."

"That is what you get for trying to be kind to the Walker family," said Caroline in a rage. "No wonder they looked more cheerful. They were planning to steal our clothes!"

Caroline and her mother cried awhile.

"Of course your father's suit had several moth holes," said Mrs. Gray at last. "And there were those places which the mice ate. And some of the petticoats were a little mildewed."

Caroline was still boiling with anger.

"But to think that they were stolen!" she said. "How could they do it and not be seen?"

"Perhaps they are more clever than they seemed," sighed Mrs. Gray. "They must have wanted those clothes very much, Caroline. And, of course, we never wore them; we only kept them."

"But they were stolen from us!" cried Caroline. "That is what makes me so angry. It makes me so angry my stomach aches!"

Mrs. Gray closed the tin trunk and pushed it back under the bed.

"We will have to pretend that they did not steal the clothes," she said. "Yes, I know the trunk is empty. I know the clothes are gone. We must pretend that we *gave* them to the Walkers. We gave them to the girls because they *needed* something pretty."

"If I could only see them I would pull their hair!" said Caroline. "I would slap their cheeks. I would step on their toes!"

"Your stomachache is getting worse," said her mother. She got up from the floor in a brisk manner.

"Come on, Caroline, there is no use in crying over old clothes. Now, if we want to take a trip the trunk is empty."

"I am glad they left the trunk for us," agreed Caroline. "Even though we never take trips."

"Tomorrow we will go to the store at Pigeon Roost," said her mother cheerfully. "We will look over the new cloth. Perhaps there will be a pretty piece of red calico which we can trim with ribbons and buttons and bows for a Sunday dress."

The very next day Mrs. Gray, Caroline, and the boys went to the store at Pigeon Roost. The boys needed new shirts, too.

12. The exciting invitation

As SOON as they got to the village they went into the Wolverene Hotel to see if the post rider had left any letters for the family.

Sure enough there was a nice, thick letter from the town in New York where Mrs. Gray's father lived. They all sat down on a bench in the hotel while Mrs. Gray opened the letter and began to read it.

"Guess what?" she cried, looking up from her reading.

"Grandfather Howard is coming to visit us?" guessed Caroline.

"No, he wants you to come and visit him," Mrs. Gray said, reading. "He is so pleased that you want to be a doctor for there have never been any woman doctors in the family."

"Caroline is not a woman yet," grumbled John, "and that is a long way for her to travel by herself."

Mrs. Gray read on.

"Grandfather Howard has thought of that. Listen: 'Travel is not so dangerous as it was three years ago. Caroline may ride on the stagecoach from Pigeon Roost to the boat landing. When she has crossed the lake we will be there to meet her. We need only to know the day she starts on the journey.'"

"Of course you won't want to go," said Robert. "You would die of homesickness."

"I do want to go," cried Caroline. "Please tell him I am coming!"

Nothing else in Pigeon Roost was as exciting as the letter had been. As Caroline and her mother looked at the beautiful new calicoes on the storekeeper's shelf she would imagine herself wearing one of them in the fine city of Cooperstown, where Grandfather Howard lived.

"Your grandmother loves to have tea parties," Mrs. Gray told her daughter. "She has beautiful dishes and silverware. The girls and ladies wear such pretty clothes."

"It will be fun to go to tea parties with girls and have many girls my own age for friends," thought Caroline. Most of her life she had had only boys around her.

As the family sat down in the dining room of the Wolverene Hotel, Caroline and her mother kept talking about the visit. They could hardly eat their dinner.

The hotelkeeper's wife was a fine cook but a rather sloppy housekeeper. She brought in big platters and dishes of meat, potatoes, beans, and other things and set them down on the bare boards. Chickens walked through the dining room and gobbled up pieces of bread which fell on the floor. Her two pet goats made themselves at home with the guests, too.

Most people who ate in the hotel paid little attention to their table manners. They gobbled their food and spilled part of it. They talked in loud voices with their mouths full. They reached in front of

each other and grabbed food from the dishes and platters.

"It will not be like this at your grandparents' home in New York," said Mrs. Gray. "Your grandparents eat in a quiet, well-mannered way. Their dining room has beautiful furniture and the table is covered with a white cloth. They have servants to pass the dishes and see that you get what you want."

Henry reached across the table for the meat platter and took a great big turkey leg in his hand.

"I am glad it is Caroline and not me who is going there," he said, tearing off big bites of the meat and talking with his mouth full. "I hate having people to spy on me while I eat!"

"It will be fun to visit so many relatives," said Caroline. She had two sets of grandparents back in New York. The Howard grandparents lived in Cooperstown. The Grays lived in Gray's Crossing. The two towns were only about twenty miles apart.

There would be aunts and uncles and cousins galore.

Caroline's family had lived at Gray's Crossing before they came to Michigan. Caroline could remember Grandfather Gray's beautiful big white house.

She could remember the carpets on the floors and the pictures on the walls and the beautiful furniture and dishes.

"It will be a nuisance walking on those carpets and eating from those thin dishes," said John. "What if you would break some of the dishes?"

"Or what if you would spill something on the fine carpet," said David, "a bottle of medicine, maybe?"

Robert patted one of the goats and gave her a bread crust spread with molasses.

"It will be lonely for you in those fine houses," he said. "I doubt that you will ever see a goat or a chicken or even a cat in the dining room. "Of course, a dog would not be allowed on those carpets!"

13. The problem of Spook

CAROLINE looked at her mother in a worried way, but Mrs. Gray was busy reading the letter again and did not notice the look.

"Spook will miss you," said Steven kindly. "But I will try to look after him."

By this time Caroline was almost crying and her mother spoke sharply to the boys.

"Stop talking with your mouths full," she said. "Besides, Caroline has not yet gone to New York. We must see what her father thinks about it."

Mr. Gray surprised them all. He thought it was a fine thing for Caroline to go for a visit.

"Of course, I will hate losing my only girl for several weeks," he said. "But Michigan is pretty rough for a girl. A visit in town might be a fine thing for you."

Grandfather Howard had written that he could teach Caroline many things about being a doctor. She could come to his office whenever she wished and look at all the medicines and the knives and the books with their interesting pictures. And she could go with him when he traveled around to visit the sick, once in a while.

"When you told me you wanted to be a doctor, that gave me the idea for you to come back here for a visit," Grandfather Howard wrote. "Now I can hardly wait."

"That will be another step toward my goal in life," Caroline told her mother as she helped with the breakfast next morning. "Think of all the things you learned from Grandfather Howard before you married Father. He can teach me all those things."

"By this time he knows many new things," said Mrs. Gray, smiling. "No doubt he will show you the skeleton in his office and tell you the names of all its bones."

Mrs. Gray laughed, remembering when she was Caroline's age.

"The skeleton was lots of fun because it was so scary-looking," she told Caroline. "My brothers knew how to pull strings and make it dance. We called it the Galloping Ghost! You will have fun with the Galloping Ghost!"

"I suppose I will," answered Caroline slowly. One thought leads to another, and the thought of a dancing ghost led to the thought of a wailing spook. And that led to a very unhappy thought.

Caroline was very quiet all the rest of that day. When her mother began talking about dress patterns and ruffles and buttons she said nothing, and looked rather downhearted.

"I am glad we found this pink calico," said Mrs. Gray. "Your Grandfather Howard always liked pink for girls' dresses."

"I may not go after all," said Caroline suddenly. Her mother looked at her in amazement.

"Why, Caroline," she said. "What happened? Are you scared at the thought of the Galloping Ghost?"

"I am thinking about Spook," answered Caroline. "I do not want to go away and leave him!"

"You will not need to leave him," said Mrs. Gray cheerfully. "Many people take their dogs on the stagecoach. And he can sleep in the old doghouse under the linden tree in my father's backyard."

The boys discouraged the idea of Caroline's taking Spook with her when they heard about it.

"Remember that Spook's owner marked him with a gold-colored earring," said John. "Suppose he would meet you and Spook someday out there in New York and would recognize his dog."

"Many people come to a doctor's office," added Henry. "They come from far and wide. You would be almost sure to meet the people who lost Spook."

Robert had a frightening thought, too.

"Those people might think you had stolen their dog," he said. "Not only would they take Spook away from you, but they might have you put into prison for stealing their dog."

"I did not steal their dog!" cried Caroline angrily. "I saved his life by pulling him out of the marsh."

"But can you prove it?" asked John. "Spook is not able to talk and nobody would ever guess that he was once half-starved, covered with mud, and loaded with wood ticks!"

"If I were you, Caroline, I think I would leave the dog here," advised Steven. "We will take good care of him and try to keep him from being too lonesome for you."

"I would like to claim him as my dog until you come back," requested David, smoothing Spook's silky ears.

"Of course by the time you get back he will not remember you any more and he will be a boys' dog but you need not worry for we will be very kind to him and train him to hunt rabbits," promised Robert.

"Sometimes I think you don't want me to go visit Grandfather Howard," cried Caroline angrily. "I think you are trying to discourage me. But try away; it will do you no good! I am going to make a visit!"

She tossed her head and got up from the bench where she had been sitting.

"Come on, Spook. You and I will go for a long walk all by ourselves."

But she had only walked a few steps away from the house with the dog trotting happily behind her when her mother called.

"Come back, Caroline. The pink dress is ready for you to try on."

Most of Caroline's clothes were too small or too tight or too faded and shabby for her to take on a journey to New York. Her mother was determined that she should be nicely dressed so there was lots of sewing to be done.

The boys complained a good deal because Caroline and her mother spent so much time with the dressmaking.

"Ruffles and buttons, bows and sashes, pink calico, green muslin, petticoats, and pinafores," grumbled Henry. "That is all we hear or see."

John looked with disgust at the sewing things spread all around. "You can hardly take a step without getting tangled up in thread or scratched with pins," he grumbled. "What a nuisance a girl can be!"

"Who has time to make a cranberry pie or a maple molasses cake or a good Indian pudding any more?" growled Henry, stepping over some sewing to get to the cupboard. He found a cold sausage cake and a piece of dry gingerbread, which he ate hungrily.

"What a good time we will have when this is a family of only boys," he said, biting first on the sausage and then on the hard gingerbread. "Thank goodness boys do not need a lot of fancy clothes and there will be more time for your mother to cook good meals."

It gave Caroline a strange, uncomfortable feeling when the boys talked in that way. She imagined the family sitting around the table eating a good dinner. There would be a cake which she had not baked. There would be pudding which she had not stirred. Spook would sit close to somebody's feet but they would not be her feet.

She told everybody at school, at church, and wherever she went about the visit she was going to make.

"I am going away for a visit," she said over and over and over to one person after another.

Steven scolded her.

"You are getting worse than Mr. Nicholson," he said. "He was always talking about what he was going to do."

"Always bragging, always bragging," growled Henry as they walked home from school one day. "Why must you say it over and over, 'I am going away for a visit'?"

He gnawed at a hard piece of cornbread from his lunch pail.

"A person would think you were a parrot or that everybody was a dunce so you have to say the same thing over and over."

Robert and David joined with him, talking in high squawking voices like parrots:

"I am going away for a visit!"

"Girls and women like to talk. It is their nature," said Steven kindly.

But Caroline had a reason which she did not tell the boys. She said that to encourage herself. Every evening and every morning she touched the gold-colored buttons on her snakeskin bag and reminded herself:

"I am going away for a visit. I *am* going away for a visit. Yes, I am, I am, I am!"

If she did not remind herself often and promise herself often she might back out. There were so many things that made it hard to go away for a visit.

Brother Carpenter had thought it was fine for her to go.

"Everybody needs to travel and see something of the world," he said, "though you will be greatly missed by me and all my sheep and lambs."

"I *am* going away for a visit," said Caroline to herself.

THE DAY OF SMALL THINGS

14. Golden thoughts

WHEN the traveling peddler came by one day he had something special among the soaps and salves and ribbons of his pack.

"I hear you are going away for a visit," he said to Caroline. "I have just the thing for you."

He held out a small white book for the family to look at. It was a very pretty book with a blue silk cover decorated with golden birds and pink flowers.

"Just the thing for a young lady who is going away on a visit," he repeated. "The name of it is *Golden Thoughts*," he said, pointing to the title.

"I can read," answered Caroline, taking the little

book in her hands. "I already have three books of my own."

When she opened the blue silk covers she saw it was only empty white pages with no stories or pictures.

"It is an album," the peddler told them. "Each of your friends writes a beautiful thought on one of these pages. When you are away you can read the thoughts and you will not be homesick."

"And also your new friends can write in it so you will not forget them," added Mrs. Gray. "I think this is a nice going-away gift, Caroline."

"It is a fine gift," agreed Caroline's father. "We will buy it."

The peddler took the money for the album and without even waiting to be asked he wrote on the first page:

"Go east, go west, but home's best."

"That means no matter how far you travel it is always good to get back home," the peddler explained. He signed his name with many scrolls and flourishes: "Theophiles Gildersnapper."

"I have no home except my peddler's cart," he said, rather sadly.

"Some people who have good homes will not stay in them," said Robert in a rather angry, loud voice, looking at Caroline. "Some people are nothing but runaways."

Mr. Gray quickly put an end to any quarrel that might have started by asking Robert if he wanted to go out and sit in the barn.

When she went to school, Caroline took the album so that her friends there could write golden thoughts in it. Most of them had no golden thoughts and just wrote their names crowded on one page.

"I want a whole page for your thought," Caroline told Brother Carpenter. Brother Carpenter knew many songs, poems, Bible verses, and great thoughts. She expected something very special from him. "I will often be reading your golden thought while I am away on my visit."

"Then I must be sure that it is a very fine thought and one that you should remember," said the preacher. He waited a long while before writing his golden thought on the white page:

"Despise not the day of small things," he wrote, at last.

Caroline was just a little disappointed by Brother Carpenter's thought. For one thing, she was not sure what it meant. Besides, it was great things she really wanted to think about, not small things.

Caroline and her uncles talked about this on the way home from school.

"He knew you were a woman and a small woman and he was reminding you," explained John.

"He wanted to remind you that a woman should

spend her day in small, useful jobs like cooking and mending," said Henry, hunting around in his lunch box for something left over to eat.

Steven added his thought:

"Brother Carpenter is a man who thinks small things are important. See how many times he takes care of the sick, or sings for the downhearted, or cleans house for the newcomers!"

"Women's work," declared Robert, tossing his head and stamping along. "He will never go down in history by doing women's work!"

He snorted and pranced ahead and it was easy to see he imagined he was a great general riding a fiery horse and leading the way to battle.

"All the same," Caroline said to Steven, "when the people around here are sick or in trouble they would rather have Brother Carpenter come and cook soup for them than to have the King of England visiting."

15. Brother Carpenter's new job

A DAY or so later, three important-looking men came to the school to visit. It was not really the school they cared about, they just wanted to talk to Brother Carpenter.

"We have heard that you are a great leader and a fine speaker and have many friends in Michigan," said one of the men.

"We have another job for you," a second man said. "We want you to come to the city and be one of our lawmakers."

"A man as smart as you should be in the state capital, doing big things," said the third visitor. "You are too big a man for such a small place as Pigeon Roost."

Brother Carpenter thanked them for this great honor but said he was not yet ready to leave Pigeon Roost.

"I have many sheep around here who need me," said the preacher. "They might give up if I went off and left them."

"You have a chance to be a great man at the state capital," said one of the visitors. "Who knows—you might even be the governor someday."

But nothing the men would say could make Brother Carpenter change his mind. The men rode off looking disappointed. They were sure that Brother Carpenter was meant for bigger things.

"I am so thankful that Brother Carpenter would not leave," said Caroline, as they walked home after school. "I would hate to see him go away!"

"Why do you care?" answered John crossly. "You yourself are going away—if you ever get started."

"I will be coming back," said Caroline. "And while I am away, I like to think of Brother Carpenter being here to look after everything."

Caroline was about ready to start on her journey.

The new clothes were finished and laid carefully in the tin trunk. Any time now the trunk was ready to be loaded on the wagon and taken over to the hotel at Pigeon Roost, where the stagecoach would pick it up.

Things kept happening to delay her start. Henry got a frightful toothache and could eat nothing except a certain kind of soup which Caroline made.

"Would you go away and leave me to starve?" he roared, putting his hand to first one side of his jaw and then the other. Henry had never had a toothache in his life until the very day before Caroline was to leave.

"I can wait a few days till the tooth doctor comes to Pigeon Roost and can pull the tooth," agreed Caroline.

Then Caroline's mother got one of her bad headaches.

"I think it is caused by worrying," she said, drinking the fennel blossom tea which Caroline made for her. "I keep dreaming that you get lost on the way to New York. I dream that the steamboat was wrecked, or a robber stopped the stagecoach."

"People always have bad dreams when they are

sick," said Caroline. "Remember those sick little twins, how they imagined I was being mean to them?"

Caroline's father came in the house in time to hear this conversation. He was limping because his horse, Snort, had accidentally stepped on his foot.

"Caroline is young and small for a long trip alone," he said. "I have been thinking. If she will wait a few days longer until my foot is well and I can spare one of the boys, perhaps Steven could go with her."

Caroline was delighted.

"I would gladly wait several months if Steven could go with me," she cried. "I would feel much safer."

"We will see what Steven says," her father decided. "He may not wish to leave school."

But Steven was pleased at the idea of going to New York.

"If I go with you, you will not need to take Spook," he said. "I will be all the protection you need."

"I will look after Firecracker for you, Steven," offered Robert. "He will not even miss you!"

"Does nobody care about my toothache?" roared Henry. "Without Caroline's soup I will starve to death and it is a terrible thing to die of starvation!"

"Tomorrow I will begin on some new shirts for Steven," promised Mrs. Gray. "I will have time to make some more clothes for Caroline, too."

Caroline felt happier about the visit now that Steven was going with her. Her mother finished two more new dresses and three new petticoats for Caroline and started in on a new shirt for Steven.

But the very evening when she was putting the finishing touches to Steven's new shirt, Brother Carpenter came riding by.

"There is a new family back in Wolf Forest that is having a very hard time," he said. "All are sick with the shivers and shakes and the poor old grandfather is about to die."

"Were you wanting me to go to their home and help take care of them?" said Mrs. Gray with a sigh.

"Not this time," answered the preacher. "I myself am going, for they need a strong pair of hands, and a great deal of cheering up. I will go take care of them if Steven will teach school in my place."

Steven hesitated. "Will they be needing you for a long time?" he asked.

"That I cannot say," answered the preacher. "It

might be a good while. They are in great need of help."

"I will teach the school for you," promised Steven. "We will put off our trip for a few days."

Mrs. Gray packed a basket of food for the sick family and Brother Carpenter rode down the Wolf Forest road singing in a resounding voice:

"Go to the pillow of disease
Where night gives no repose;
And on the cheek where sickness preys,
Bid health to plant the rose!"

"I do wonder what the people around here would do without Brother Carpenter," said Mrs. Gray, looking after him with a smile.

"He is a great man," added Mr. Gray. "No job is too small for him!"

"I hope you are not too disappointed at having to put off your visit," Caroline's mother said.

Caroline did not feel too disappointed. "It will be fun to have Steven for a schoolteacher," she answered. "What a surprise for Josiebell Jones and the other big girls when they see Steven up there in the teacher's place!"

16. At Wolf Forest

SEVERAL days went by. Mrs. Gray got over her headache and Mr. Gray could walk without limping. The tooth doctor at Pigeon Roost could not find a single hole in any of Henry's teeth.

"We could start most any day if Steven did not have to teach school," said Caroline. Steven, however, really enjoyed being a schoolteacher and the scholars enjoyed having such a young, lively teacher.

Brother Carpenter was still busy at Wolf Forest. The poor old grandfather had not yet died and needed care. Two other families had come to make their homes in that lonely, dreary forest and they needed help.

"How would you like to ride back to Wolf Forest and see how Brother Carpenter is getting along?" Mrs. Gray asked Steven one Saturday. "I have done a big baking today and you can take some fresh bread with you."

Steven agreed.

"Caroline can go with me," he said. "We will talk over our plans for the visit as we ride through the woods."

Caroline and Steven rode off together, Steven on Firecracker and Caroline on old Dolly. Spook trotted along behind old Dolly.

Caroline carried her snakeskin bag over her arm. It was well stuffed with packages of medicinal herbs and a little extra food Henry had put in.

It was easy for Caroline to imagine that she was a grown-up woman doctor on her way to see some sick person. It was easy to imagine that old Dolly was a prancing black horse, snorting and pawing.

The snakeskin bag had become a large leather saddlebag stuffed with medicine for every sickness.

Behind her came her faithful dog, ready to kill anybody who dared bother the woman doctor.

Firecracker kept a little ahead for he was too young and frisky to keep step with fat old Dolly.

Caroline tossed her head back as she had often seen Brother Carpenter do and began to sing at the top of her voice:

> "Go to the pillow of disease
>   Where night gives no repose;
> And on the cheek where sickness preys,
>   Bid health to plant the rose!"

Old Dolly twitched one ear and walked a little faster. Spook looked all around in surprise.

"How glad the people will be when they hear me singing," thought Caroline happily, and sang even more loudly:

> "Go where the friendless stranger lies;
>   To perish is his doom;
> Snatch from the grave his closing eyes,
>   And bring his blessing home!"

Steven turned Firecracker around and came back to Caroline.

"Good gracious!" he cried. "How you shriek! At first I thought it was a wildcat, coming through the trees!"

But he laughed as he spoke, so Caroline felt sure he did not really mistake her singing for a wildcat's yowls.

It was a long ride to the clearing in Wolf Forest. They went by Wolf Hill, where Mr. Nicholson had talked at the house-raising and they wondered what had happened to the schoolteacher.

"I wonder something else," said Caroline. "I wonder what if he had not called on me that morning. What if I had not spoken up and told my goal?"

"Women should keep silent most of the time," said Steven kindly. "A talkative woman is worse than a crowing hen. But there are exceptions."

Caroline held her peace, but she thought her thought.

"If I had kept silent that morning things would have been different. I would not have this snakeskin bag. I would not have my dog, Spook. I would not be getting ready to go away for a visit so far away!"

They found Brother Carpenter out in the clearing hanging blankets and things on the bushes. He had just finished the wash and was delighted to see Steven and Caroline. He had been singing as he hung up the blankets and he stopped only to say, "Welcome, welcome!"

"What a blessing that you came!" he cried. "To-morrow is preaching day at Pigeon Roost and I

should be there. Yet I do not like to leave these poor, sick, lonely, frightened people all alone."

He waved his hand proudly about.

"Wolf Forest is growing," he said. "See, there are three families here. If they do not give up and go away we can soon have another fine little town here in Michigan. Already I have picked out the place for the church."

He led the way into one of the cabins.

"These strong young people have come to look after you while I preach tomorrow," he said cheerfully. "Steven can do the outdoor work. Caroline is a good cook and has a way with the sick!"

Steven opened his mouth to speak.

"I was sure I could count on you to help," the preacher said happily, not giving Steven a chance to speak and say that they had only come for a short call.

The cabin had only two rooms. In one of them was the sick old grandfather, who had not yet died, and the couple who were just getting over the shivers and shakes. It was a gloomy, dark place but seemed more cheerful when Brother Carpenter was in it, singing and talking.

Brother Carpenter soon rode away, promising to tell Mr. and Mrs. Gray where they were and to be back early Monday morning so Steven and Caroline could go to school.

"We even forgot to ask him when he is coming back to be the teacher," said Steven.

He built up the fire and put fresh water in the cooking pot. Caroline got busy making mush.

Spook came in and curled up quietly under a bench.

While the mush bubbled, Caroline looked in her snakeskin bag for medicinal herbs. She found some quinine bark and some sassafras root. There were also several lumps of maple sugar, for Henry had told her she should always carry something good to eat in case she got lost in the woods.

She mixed a nice bowl of medicine and carried some in to the sick couple. The poor old grandfather was too sick to drink any of it, but the man and woman gladly drank it.

"This is like having a tea party," sighed the woman, drinking the dark, sweet, bitter brew. "It has been a long time since I went to a tea party and had a nice visit with ladies. Tell me, do they ever have ladies' tea parties in Michigan?"

"Oh yes," answered Caroline. "We have many nice parties. We have house-raisings, and quiltings, and sewing bees—"

"If I could just have one more nice party with lots of ladies to talk to and some good tea to drink, it would be better than medicine—even this fine medicine you have made."

"I will tell my mother," promised Caroline. "I myself am going away for a visit, but my mother will have the party for you."

The woman looked disappointed.

"I was hoping you could come to the tea party. A nice young girl is a great help at a tea party."

"Once we had a girl of our own," said the man sadly. "She ate green apples and died when she was only three years old."

"She looked a great deal like you," added the woman. A tear fell into her teacup. "She would have been about your age if she had not eaten those green apples."

"Have some more tea," said Caroline, dipping

from the pot. She added an extra lump of maple sugar.

"I am going to be a doctor when I grow up," she told the sick couple. "I will have medicine to cure the sickness caused by eating green apples."

The woman drank the tea, which was bitter as gall and thick as molasses.

"It makes me feel better just to have you here," she said. "Brother Carpenter is a grand man and quite good at housekeeping but nothing is so nice as a young girl around the house."

GOOD LIKE MEDICINE

17. Good news and horrible news

ALMOST before sunrise Monday morning Brother Carpenter was back. The old grandfather had not yet died, and the sick couple seemed quite a bit better.

"I knew you could help them," said the preacher. "You have a way with the sick, Caroline!"

"We forgot to ask him when he was coming back to teach school," Caroline said as she and Steven were on their way back.

"He will not be back to teach school," Steven said, rather gloomily. "He told me as we were feeding the horses. So we will have to wait a few weeks longer."

"Grandfather Howard has already waited several

months," said Caroline. "He may think I am not coming."

"Then he will have a happy surprise when you do come," Steven returned.

Caroline was glad when the school day was over and she was back home. Her mother had cooked a fine supper to welcome her and Steven.

Brother Carpenter had told the people at church that he would not be able to teach school any more as he had too many new sheep to look after.

"I hope I will not get too big for my new clothes before Steven and I start on our trip," said Caroline.

"I have good news for you," Mr. Gray told Caroline. "The hotelkeeper's cousin will soon be coming through Pigeon Roost. He is a surveyor who travels around measuring the land. He once lived in New York State near the town where Grandfather Howard lives. Grandfather Howard was once his family doctor."

"I would rather wait for Steven," said Caroline.

"The surveyor may be a little disappointed," said Mrs. Gray. "He has a nice little wagon big enough to hold your trunk. And his wife likes to travel, so she always goes with him and would be company for you."

"Steven and I have made all our plans for the trip," said Caroline, "but I will not forget to thank the surveyor if he stops for me."

Another week went by and when Caroline and the boys came home from school one evening, the surveyor had come. He had already been told that Caroline would not be going with him, but he was staying for supper and the night.

When Caroline walked into the house followed by Spook there was a great surprise. Spook barked excitedly and the surveyor and his wife looked amazed.

"Where did you find our lost dog, Prince?" cried the surveyor's wife. "He has been missing for months."

"We lost him on our last trip through Pigeon County," said the surveyor.

"He was lost in the marsh. I rescued him," said Caroline. Spook left the visitors and came running back to her.

"He came all the way from England," said the surveyor's wife. "My father gave him to me for a wedding present when I came to this wild, dangerous land."

Caroline was feeling sadder and sadder. All the boys looked as if they were at a funeral.

"I suppose you felt very bad when you lost your dog," said Caroline, who could hardly keep from crying.

"Oh, I wept for days and days and days," said the young woman. "I hated to tell my father we had lost his gift."

Caroline and the boys did not feel much like eating, even though there was a good company supper.

David sat with tears running down his cheeks and Robert looked very angry.

"It is all your fault!" he scolded Caroline when supper was over and the ladies were washing dishes while the men talked about surveying. "You see what happens because of your silly ideas. If you had not been going to visit your grandfather because he is a doctor, these people would never have come by here and they would have gone on thinking that Spook was dead. Now they will take him away."

"They cannot prove he is their dog," declared John fiercely.

But they could prove it. The young woman had pushed back the hair on Spook's ear and touched the shiny earring.

"My father put this in his ear," she said.

Even Spook seemed worried. He would run over to the visitors and whine a little as if he were glad to see them. But immediately he would run back to Caroline and curl up at her feet.

"It's hard to know which of us the dog really belongs to," said the surveyor in a worried way.

The young woman kept saying over and over to Caroline, "I can never thank you enough for saving Prince's life. My father will thank you, too!"

Morning came. The surveyor and his wife got ready to go. The surveyor took several gold dollars from his purse and handed them to Caroline. "Here is a small reward for saving our dog," he said.

But Caroline would not take the money. She did not want money for saving Spook.

The surveyor looked at Caroline's face and at his wife's sad face.

"This is worse than trying to divide a homestead in two parts," he said. "It is a hard problem to decide. Who is going to decide?"

"Why not let Prince decide?" said his wife. "He can come with us or he can stay with you and he can be the one to decide."

The surveyor got into the wagon and his wife got in beside him. The dog looked at them and then at Caroline. Everybody waited.

"Be sure to come over to the big cherry fair at

Cherrystone in August," called the surveyor. He shook the lines and his horses began to move.

Then Spook gave a little whine and ran out to the wagon. He jumped in and settled down in the back of the wagon.

Caroline wanted to call, "Come back, Spook, come back. Remember I saved your life!"

But she had promised to let Spook decide and she must keep her promise.

Caroline and her uncles went off to school feeling rather lonely.

"Still," said Steven, trying to be cheerful, "think how we might have felt if one of us had been lost and found again."

"Where is your brown dog, Spook, Caroline?" asked one of the other scholars. Caroline answered:

"It is too long a story to tell."

"And too sad, also," added Robert.

18. A dark and scary night

SCHOOL would be out in two more weeks. Again Caroline and Steven began talking over the plans for their trip.

"Perhaps I can see Spook again," sighed Caroline. "Maybe the surveyor and his wife will be traveling through Cooperstown while we are there."

"A surveyor never stays in one place very long," Mr. Gray said. "Remember, their home is *now* in Cherrystone, where the cherry fair is held.

"I am sure my father will get another dog for Caroline," said Mrs. Gray. "He always had a dog that went with him to see the sick. He will find a good dog for Caroline."

"But still it will not be a dog that I rescued from the marsh and snatched from the grave when he was about to perish," answered Caroline rather mournfully.

"One more week and we will be starting," said Steven, when several days had gone by. He seemed even more eager than Caroline to make the trip.

"It will be fun to see all my other brothers again," he said.

When he got home he went out to the pasture and got Firecracker.

"I will take a short ride before supper," he told the family. "The colt needs to stretch his legs."

"If you were not going along with Steven, he could take Firecracker to New York," said Robert, as his big brother galloped away on the red colt. "He could make the trip on horseback easily. But since he has to look after you, I will look after Firecracker while he is away."

Caroline went on into the house and began helping her mother put the supper on the table.

"Brother Carpenter came by this afternoon," Mrs. Gray told her daughter. "That poor old grandfather finally died. Brother Carpenter had a nice funeral for him and sang several songs. He hopes that we can soon have a tea party for those people, maybe in about ten days."

"I will be away by that time," said Caroline, getting the bowl of apple butter from the cupboard. "But you can still have the tea party."

"That lady especially hoped that you could come," said Mrs. Gray. "She said you did her more good than medicine."

"I suppose we could wait and start the day after the tea party," agreed Caroline.

The supper was on the table and everybody except Steven was in the house, hungry and ready to eat.

"Where did Steven go?" wondered Mrs. Gray. "My stew is getting cold. The tea will be bitter."

Steven did not come. It began to rain and was almost dark.

"I am starving," complained Henry. "Let's eat. When Steven is riding on Firecracker he forgets that other people may be hungry."

"If *I* went out for a ride just at suppertime and

stayed so late, *I* would not expect the family to wait supper for me," declared John, looking hungrily at the Indian pudding on the table.

So the family sat down and ate. Caroline was worried. She did not think Steven would be so late without a good reason.

It was raining a little harder and getting darker all the time.

"I am sure something has happened to Steven," declared Caroline, pushing aside her bowl of Indian pudding. "I think we should go out and hunt for Steven."

"Which way would we go?" asked John.

Henry asked, "How could we see the way to go?"

"I will light our way with those torches we made by soaking pine sticks in grease last year," said Caroline.

Mr. Gray got the greasy torches from the storeroom and lighted them from the fireplace. He told Caroline she had better stay with her mother but Caroline insisted on going. She took the snakeskin bag with its salve, smelling salts, and other remedies. Henry put in a big piece of bread. "Steven might be starving by this time," he said.

As Caroline put the things into her bag her fingers touched the willow whistle which Steven had made for her. She had almost thrown it away when Spook went off with the surveyor, but had decided to keep it just for memory's sake.

Now she was glad she did. The willow whistle was clear and loud. Steven would surely hear it.

Out they all went into the rainy darkness with their blowing torches, each torch protected by one of Mrs. Gray's tin pans.

They went out to the pasture where Steven had got on Firecracker. Caroline blew the willow whistle with all her might. Her father and the boys called at the tops of their voices. They went slowly through the darkness.

Suddenly Caroline cried, "Stop! Listen!"

When they listened, they could hear the sound of another whistle, coming from somewhere out in the darkness. It was not so loud and strong as Caroline's. It was a little bit weak.

"But it's Steven, blowing the willow whistle he made for Spook!"

They followed the faint sound through the windy darkness and presently they could see Firecracker standing there. He whinnied softly and it was almost as if he were saying:

"Thank goodness you came at last!"

Steven was lying on the ground. He tried to tell them what had happened.

"An owl flew out, right across Firecracker's nose. He jumped and threw me off. It wasn't his fault, I wasn't watching."

Steven's head had hit a fallen tree trunk and he had been lying there unconscious. He had waked up when he heard the calling and whistling. He was lucky he still had his own willow whistle. He was too weak to shout and he could not get up.

Mr. Gray and the boys managed to lift Steven to Firecracker's back while Caroline held the torches. Slowly they made the short trip across the pasture back to the house. Steven had once again gone to sleep and he groaned now and then.

But Caroline felt like singing in spite of her worry over Steven. Suppose they had not found Steven in the darkness? Suppose he had had to lie on the wet ground all night long? Suppose a wolf had come out of the woods—there were still a few wolves around Pigeon County.

"But we have snatched him from the grave. We are bringing him home."

Caroline marched ahead lighting the way. Her torch was still burning because she had kept it covered with a tin bread pan. She hummed softly under her breath as she splashed along.

"What are you singing about?" grumbled John. "Steven may be dying. It is a dangerous thing to have a horse throw you."

"How lucky that it happened so close to home!" answered Caroline, and went on singing under her breath.

They helped Steven into the house and laid him on the bed. Mrs. Gray felt him carefully to see if any bones were broken.

There was a huge bump on his head and a bad cut on his arm where it had scraped against a broken tree limb. He groaned and cried "Ouch!" when Mrs. Gray touched his back.

"There will be no more schoolteaching for you this year," said his sister-in-law. "You will have to be very quiet for a while."

Steven sneezed about a dozen or so times. Caroline had already dipped up a cup of water from the kettle and put some tonic into it.

She helped her mother bandage the cut arm and put a poultice on the bumped head.

"What a day this has been!" she cried, when Steven was safely cared for and things settled down. "What an exciting evening!"

But the excitement of the day was not yet over. There was a scratching and a whining at the door and when Mr. Gray opened it, Spook walked in.

He was wet and muddy and a little lame. His beautiful brown coat was full of burrs and ticks. But he was wild with joy to see all the family again, especially Caroline.

Caroline forgave him for going off with the surveyor. She hugged him, not minding the wetness and the mud; the burrs and even the ticks.

"He made up his mind and he has come back home," cried Caroline almost weeping with joy.

Henry hurried to bring Spook a plate of stewed squirrel and dumplings, while David and Robert began taking off the burrs and ticks.

"I think Spook has been reading Caroline's album," declared John, forgetting to be gloomy. He quoted the peddler's golden thought:

"Go east, go west, but home's best!"

"Wasn't it lucky we held on to those willow whistles?" said Steven hoarsely from the bed. He sneezed several times. "Very lucky," he mumbled between sneezes.

"I always thought maybe Spook would come back," said Caroline. "I always kept hoping."

19. The postponed journey

ONCE more the trip to New York was put off, for Steven's back bothered him and he had to lie down a great deal.

Summer came. Mr. Gray and the younger boys planted corn. Caroline and her mother planted beans and peas and potatoes.

The wild strawberries ripened and Caroline and her mother were very busy picking them.

The tin trunk, packed with Caroline's pretty new clothes, was packed and ready for her trip.

"When we are not so busy and Steven is strong again, you will be going away for your trip," said

Caroline's mother. "You will be ready to go on a minute's notice."

Caroline and her mother walked in the woods picking the herbs and roots and berries for medicine. They were not afraid to go away back where the mayapple and ginseng grew because Spook stayed close behind them.

One day a letter came from Grandfather Howard. He was disappointed that Caroline had not yet come for the visit but was cheerful about it.

"You are still young and will still have time for the visit before you grow up and marry and become too busy for visits."

"He has forgotten that I am going to be a doctor when I grow up," said Caroline.

Mrs. Gray read on.

"Since Caroline is not coming your mother and I have decided to take a trip back to England," Dr. Howard wrote. "We have long been wanting to go, but were waiting for Caroline's visit to be over!"

"Hurrah!" cried David. John and Robert and Henry joined in, "Hurrah, hurrah, hurrah! Now Caroline can stay at home and make strawberry shortcake every day."

Strawberry shortcake was a delicious new dish which Brother Carpenter had learned about from one of his sheep. He had showed Caroline how to make it.

"Why do I feel so happy, I wonder," Caroline asked herself. "I should be feeling disappointed. But I am happy. I want to do something exciting."

She went outside and ran a few races with Spook. That was fun, but not exciting.

"May I ride old Dolly back to the marsh and take some of our young green peas to Mrs. Merrill?" she asked. The marsh home no longer seemed so far away and she was no longer afraid to go past the marsh.

Mrs. Merrill was glad to see her. "You are better than medicine," she said. She looked a little down-hearted. "I have not had any fun for a long time," she said. "In Boston, where I lived, there were many things to do. There were dances and parties and concerts and the opera. How I loved the opera! And there were fairs, the most fun of all!"

She shelled peas with a faraway look in her eyes.

"House-raisings are nice and quilting bees are useful," she sighed. "But if I could only go to the opera one more time! Or to a fair, with fire-eaters and marionettes!"

Suddenly Caroline remembered something so exciting that she let her bowl of peas fall to the floor.

"The cherry fair!" she cried. "The cherry fair at Cherrystone. Let's all go to the cherry fair!"

She did not wait to eat with the Merrills. She got on old Dolly and rode back home as fast as the lazy mare would travel.

"The cherry fair!" she cried, rushing into the house. "Remember the fair at Cherrystone. Soon the cherries will be getting ripe!"

Most of the family had forgotten that the surveyor had invited them to the cherry fair.

Mr. Gray said he had lots of work to do, and Mrs. Gray said she had lots of work to do, and Steven said his back ached too much.

But Caroline had made up her mind. She would not stop talking about the cherry fair until her father agreed to go.

20. A fine, exciting fair

"AT LAST I can wear my new clothes," said Caroline. She opened the tin trunk and picked out the prettiest dresses. It was a good thing, too, for even now the dresses were a wee bit short on her.

The boys, except Steven, rode horses. So there was room in the wagon for the Merrill family.

"Isn't this fun?" cried Mrs. Merrill, who looked years younger today. "I haven't gone to a fair since we left Massachusetts."

Even the long journey through the woods to Cherrystone was like a picnic. Only Steven was rather gloomy. He did not like having to ride in the wagon. He did not like spending so much time in bed and having a backache.

As they drove into the town of Cherrystone it seemed a very exciting place. It was built by the lake and there were several boats on the lake.

The town of Cherrystone was decorated with banners and welcome signs. There were baskets of ripe red cherries everywhere. Ripe red cherries hung thick on trees which grew along the street.

There were tables along the street where you could buy good things to eat, or medicine for pains, or jewelry made of colored glass.

Most exciting were the shows. Sure enough there was a fire-eater from England. There were some dancing bears and other animals. There was a parade of horses.

Steven looked very gloomy at the sight of this parade.

"I was a better rider than any of those riders," he said. "And Firecracker was better than any of those horses."

Today Robert was riding Firecracker, who stamped and snorted as he looked at the strange sights along the street.

[175]

The surveyor and his wife were at the fair and were glad to see the Grays. They were glad to see Spook, too, but this time Spook stayed close to Caroline and did not offer to follow them.

"I have two canary birds now who go everyplace with us, riding in their cage," the young woman told Caroline.

"This is a fine, exciting fair," Mrs. Gray said.

"But you have not seen the best thing yet," the surveyor told her. "Tonight will be the show at the

opera house. People come for miles around to see it."

"I am almost too tired to go to a show," said Steven, when evening came.

The others coaxed him to go. Caroline and the boys had never seen a traveling show in an opera house. They had never been in an opera house.

The opera house, which was also a warehouse and the town hall, was crowded. The Grays and the Merrills had to sit near the back.

21. "Nothing surprises me!"

FINALLY the curtain went up and the show began.

A small, terrible-looking man came out on the stage. He had coal-black whiskers and jet-black hair. He carried a sword in one hand and a pistol in the other. He wore a fine black suit which was quite a bit too large for him.

He looked fiercely at all the people in front of him. Then he spoke in a loud, savage voice:

"The name of this show is 'The Terrible Sile Doty.' I am Sile Doty!"

Another small but fierce-looking man came out. He had a red beard and wild red hair.

"I am Sile Doty's partner," he shouted. "We are the most dreaded and dangerous criminals in Michigan!"

Two girls came out dressed in elegant clothes. One wore red taffeta and the other wore green satin.

"Those look very much like my dresses," Mrs. Gray whispered to Caroline.

The girls spoke together. "We are the wife and daughter of Sile Doty," they howled. "Our adventures will make your blood run cold!"

"Those girls sound very much like the Walker girls," Caroline whispered to her mother.

Two very small children dressed in pretty flowered dresses came out. They danced and sang a song. Their song was very sad and scary, being about two poor little orphans who were stolen away by wicked spooks in a marsh. Yet they sang cheerfully and danced gaily.

"Those clothes look just like the clothes Grandfather Gray sent for your birthday!" whispered Mrs. Gray.

Caroline answered:

"And those twins look about like the Walker twins, only much cleaner and better dressed!"

"No wonder, they are wearing better clothes!" said Mrs. Gray.

A tall man and woman came out.

"We are two brave, honest people who were robbed by Sile Doty," they wailed. "Listen to our sad tale!"

They sang a long sad song about their woes.

"It is the Walkers. It is certainly the Walker family," said the Grays to one another.

Several people looked back at them, hissing and frowning. "We want to hear the show!" they hissed.

The show was long and exciting and funny. Most of the ladies liked the twins the best. The twins sang and danced several songs.

They sang a song about a terrible adventure in the woods when wolves chased them. Just as the wolves were ready to eat them, a brave girl ran out and saved them. She killed the wolves and carried the children home in her arms. There she fed them on dainties of every kind and dressed them in silken robes.

"Black was her hair and long and fine,
The name of the girl was Caroline," they sang.

Caroline blushed, and the boys were too amazed to do more than stare.

This was a sad song and the twins sang it sadly, wiping their eyes as they sang.

"She died at the age of almost eleven;
    She is an angel now in heaven.
    She flies through the sky on golden wings,
    And as she flies she sweetly sings."

The twins sang this song so sadly and so sweetly that many ladies wiped tears from their eyes.

Everybody applauded the show. Only the Gray family forgot to applaud because they were thunder-struck with amazement.

At last the show was over and the Walker family came out and bowed.

"Tomorrow night we have a different show," said Dorcas. "It is called, 'Josiebell, the Horse Thief's Beautiful, Wicked Daughter.' I am Josiebell in the play."

They bowed again and went out the back door of the opera house. One of the important men of Cherrystone came out and invited everybody to come back to the fair tomorrow and come to the show again. He spoke very kindly of the show.

"We are lucky to have this fine traveling show for our cherry fair," he said. "Laughing is good for people. The traveling show makes people laugh and does lots of good!"

"Shall we go up and say hello to the Walkers?" asked Robert. "Shall we remind them of how they visited us and tell them that Caroline is not in heaven after all?"

"I would like to tell them that we really gave them the clothes," said Mrs. Gray, "but maybe they already think we did."

"They have forgotten their miserable life as pioneers," said Steven. "Let's not remind them of the time when they were poor and hungry and had so many fleas. Those hard days are past."

Steven had not looked so cheerful since the night he got hurt.

"This will be something to tell about when we go to New York in a few years," he said to Caroline.

Mrs. Merrill was impressed when she heard that the Walkers had once lived in her home.

"To think that our house was once the home of

such fine actors!" she said. "I am going to feel better about living there from now on."

"They need not know *everything* about the Walkers," Caroline told the boys. "Everybody needs some secrets."

At last the cherry fair was over and the family loaded up to go home. One of the Cherrystone men came to tell them good-by.

"Be sure to come back to our fair next year," he said. "The railroad will be built by that time and you can ride on the train. It travels fast, almost forty miles an hour."

He smiled pleasantly at Caroline.

"This young lady would enjoy a ride on the train," he said. "It goes fast, but we have a fine engineer. His name is Mr. Nicholson!"

"I am not really surprised, after all!" said Caroline. She patted Spook, who was standing close against her. "Almost nothing that people do surprises me," she said.

Steven looked at her. But he did not frown.

"This is my niece Caroline," he told the important man. "She is going to be a doctor."

Caroline stroked the shabby old snakeskin bag,

which hung from her arm. She smiled but kept silent.

"Yes, when Caroline grows up she is going to be a doctor," repeated the other boys in chorus. They did not sound embarrassed or angry.

They sounded very proud, as if they really enjoyed saying it.